EVERYONE KNOWS BUT YOU

EVERYONE KNOWS BUT YOU

A TALE OF MURDER ON THE MAINE COAST

THOMAS E. RICKS

PEGASUS CRIME

NEW YORK LONDON

EVERYONE KNOWS BUT YOU

Pegasus Crime is an imprint of
Pegasus Books, Ltd.
148 West 37th Street, 13th Floor
New York, NY 10018

Copyright © 2024 by Thomas E. Ricks

First Pegasus Books cloth edition June 2024

Interior design by Maria Fernandez

Map of Ryan Tapia's Maine by Gene Thorp

Library of Congress Cataloging-in-Publication Data is available.

ISBN: 978-1-63936-679-8

10 9 8 7 6 5 4 3 2 1

Printed in the United States of America
Distributed by Simon & Schuster
www.pegasusbooks.com

For they that go down to the sea in ships

PRINCIPAL CHARACTERS

Ryan Tapia: sole agent in the FBI's Bangor office, an extension of the agency's Portland branch office

Harriet Williams: agent overseeing the FBI's Portland suboffice, itself a branch of the Boston field office, and so Ryan's supervisor

Ricky Cutts: a ne'er-do-well lobsterman

Shirley Cutts: his hospitalized mother

Caleb Goodwin: leader of the Highliners, the unofficial overseers of the lobstering enterprise on Liberty Island

Hercules "Herc" Fernald: a member of the Highliners

Johnny Mac: subtribal police officer for the southern branch of the Malpense tribe, also the subtribal chief

"Peeled Paul" Soco: a member of the Malpense tribe living a hermit's existence on Big Bold Island

Absalom "Abby" Buck: island entrepreneur

Dorothy Peyton: county medical examiner

Solidarity Harrison: high-end fish marketer and Dorothy's partner

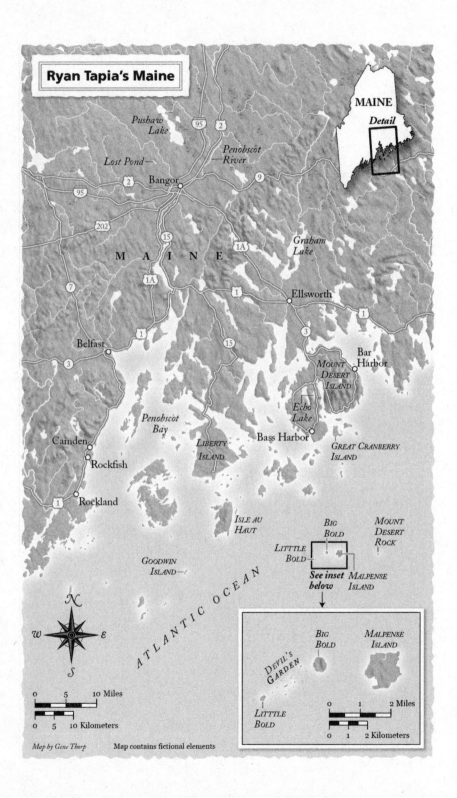

Ryan Tapia's Maine

MAINE
Detail

Pushaw
Lake
Lost Pond
Penobscot
River
Bangor
95   2
95
2
202
9
15
1A
M A I N E
Graham
Lake
1A
7
1
Ellsworth
15
1
3
Belfast
1
Mount
Desert
Island
Bar
Harbor
3
Penobscot
Bay
Echo
Lake
Camden
Liberty
Island
Bass Harbor
Great Cranberry
Island
Rockfish
Rockland
1
Isle au
Haut
Big
Bold
Mount
Desert
Rock
Litttle
Bold
Goodwin
Island
See inset
below
Malpense
Island
Devil's
Garden
Big
Bold
Malpense
Island
Litttle
Bold
0   1   2 Miles
0   1   2 Kilometers
N
W   E
S
ATLANTIC OCEAN

0   5   10 Miles
0   5   10 Kilometers

Map by Gene Thorp   Map contains fictional elements

WESTERN EAR HEADLAND,
ISLE AU HAUT, MAINE

As Ryan Tapia made his way down the far southwestern shore of Isle au Haut, his eye was drawn to the pink granite sloping down to the sea, the way it held the warm late-afternoon sunlight gleaming across the water. He still had not grown accustomed to the intense beauty of the Maine coast, with its sharp green forests, blue skies and waters, and pink rockbound shores. Its huge, unending tides, sometimes running to fifteen or twenty feet—it was all stunning. He realized, with surprise, that five months after the accident, he was beginning to enjoy nature again and perhaps to appreciate life. Or parts of it. Not people. Not at all.

After walking along the shore cliff for a half mile south of the Duck Harbor ferry landing, Ryan stopped and surveyed the scene. He reviewed the directions he had received from the law enforcement liaison officer at the Acadia National Park headquarters. He had reached what she had called "a notable notch in the cliff." He looked down into the water, and there, about five feet below him, he perceived what he had been summoned to see—a body bobbing face down in the dark green seaweed of low tide. His eye followed the slope upward, to where groves of stunted spruce and fir maintained a gnarled hold in the thin, pebble-heavy topsoil. There, also as promised, at the line between the rock and the woods, leaning against a boulder, sat the man who had been waiting for him, a national park ranger clad in the dark greens and grays of his service.

Ryan walked closer. He sniffed once and then again. There definitely was a skunky reek of marijuana in the air. Was there someone else here? He looked around and peered into the darkness of the trees. No. Ryan approached the man, who was still leaning, and saw that he was puffing on a joint. Thin gray smoke curled up around the brim of his Smokey Bear hat. He sported an untrimmed beard and a ponytail, both flecked with gray.

The ranger in turn looked Ryan up and down, taking in the sight, unusual on a remote edge of the Maine coast, of a lanky man in his thirties wearing crew cut red hair, khaki trousers, a blue oxford shirt, a blue blazer, and black shoes with rubber soles. "You the FBI man?" the ranger asked, stating the obvious. Ryan could not have looked more out of place. In rural Maine, even bankers dressed like they were going deer hunting, in jeans and flannels. The ranger's eyes were bloodshot.

Ryan nodded. He had a lot of questions, but the indolent ranger beat him to it, saying, "Had to fuck up pretty bad to get posted to Bangor, huh?"

In just four weeks of being assigned to Maine, Ryan had grown accustomed to this jibe. Upon learning that he was from the Federal Bureau of Investigation, Mainers, with their rough rustic humor, instantly would prod him verbally. He had heard it half a dozen times, the bemusement that he was not just exiled to Maine, but all the way to the Bangor office, an outpost of the Portland office, which itself was a satellite of the bureau's Boston office. The end of the line in more ways than one, he had been informed several times in a variety of ways.

"I requested the assignment," Ryan responded evenly. He didn't care to explain himself. For his part, he wanted to ask how a federal official—which the park ranger was—could smoke marijuana while in uniform and on the job, and indeed while on federal land. *But*, he reminded himself, *stick to your tasks*. That was how he had gotten through life since the accident. Each day, one foot ahead of the other. Each night, horrible dreams.

The task at hand was still floating in the seaweed down below them. "There's your man," the ranger nodded. "Haven't touched it." That "it" caught Ryan's ear. *People don't know how to talk about the dead*, he mused to himself. The ranger passed over to Ryan a gaff hook, that most useful tool of the sea, used constantly to snag lines, objects, and even, in this case, a dead person.

Ryan shuffled judiciously down the slope to the water's edge. The corpse was there, bobbing in a cleft in the rocks, face down and shirtless, but what was apparent indicated that he was likely a lobsterman. Indeed, his legs were entangled in the floating rope employed in the lobster fishery. Ryan's eye followed the line over to the rocks about twenty feet away where a red-and-white lobster buoy bobbed in the seaweed. *Probably got caught up in his own gear while pulling traps and got tugged out the stern of his boat*, Ryan thought.

Ryan took a series of photographs with his cell phone to capture the time and place: "Isle au Haut, Maine/May 23." Then he extended the aluminum shaft of the gaffer. He slipped its black plastic hook under the farther belt loop on the blue jeans the overweight dead man was still wearing and then pulled it back toward himself to flip over the body.

When he did, Ryan stepped back in surprise. The hands seemed to be moving in small, frantic ways. As they came into focus, he saw the movement in fact was made by dozens of small, white-spotted green crabs, gnawing on the flesh between the fingers. And, he saw, on the armpits and lips. All the tender parts, he thought. Much of the face had been nibbled away, along with the fingers. The eyes, which to the taste of these crabs were a soft, delicious jelly, were gone altogether, leaving deep empty sockets. It always surprised Ryan how large the human eye socket was. The vacant holes were the size of tennis balls. He pulled on yellow medical gloves and then kneeled by the body, flicked away some crabs, and checked the pockets. He could feel the cold of the late-spring seawater through the gloves, and guessed the surface temperature was about forty-seven degrees. The corpse carried neither wallet nor keys. "Who are you?" he said out loud. He was feeling misled and frustrated.

No ID, no tats, not much of a face, not much left in the way of fingerprints. Just a corpse bedecked in seaweed, crabs, and snails. All courtesy of a stoned ranger, who loomed up behind Ryan at the top of the rock notch. *Welcome to Maine*, Ryan thought, wondering yet again if he had made the right choice by asking to be posted here.

"How do we get the body out of here?" Ryan asked.

"Usual drill," the ranger said.

"Which is?"

"Not the first time a body has washed up on Isle au Haut," the ranger explained. "Usually it's some 'from-away' on a yacht, gets up in the middle of the night to pee over the side, a bit unsteady from the evening gin and tonics and the red wine with dinner, a wave rocks the hull, he loses his balance, and over the side he goes, *kersplash!*" the ranger said with surprising glee, waving his arms upward. "Even on an anchored boat, it is almost impossible to get back up, unless there's a rope ladder over the side. We call that an 'open zipper death.' The crabs love those." He chuckled at his own grim humor.

Then, more informatively, he said that he had radioed ahead to the ferry's skipper. On its next run, after it dropped all its passengers at Duck Harbor, it would swing down here and his deckhand would toss a line to them. The deckhand would pull the body in. Ryan then would oversee wrapping it in a tarp, stowing it below in the ferry, and delivering it to an ambulance already waiting at the dock on Liberty Island, the main port on this part of the coast. The ambulance in turn would drive the corpse around Penobscot Bay to the county medical examiner in Rockfish, on the west side of the bay.

Ryan was relieved. "Got it, except I don't think this will be my case," he said, standing and stretching. The body might be impossible to ID, but that did not appear to be a problem for him. A drowned lobsterman was regrettable, of course, but not of any official interest to the FBI. "Why'd your liaison call me?" he asked the ranger in genuine puzzlement.

"Because," the ranger said, "in the Park Service we do drownings. We do hikers who get lost and die of exposure. We do deaths by car accidents and rock-climbing falls. Honeymooners falling off sit-on-top kayaks and getting hypothermic. We even do dads having propane explosions at campsites. But we don't do homicide investigations."

Ryan looked at him in surprise. "What?" He had seen no indication that he had a killing on his hands.

"Check out the top of his head," the ranger said. "It's stove-in. And not by these rocks—more like something narrow and heavy, like a lead pipe or something. Someone whacked this guy but good."

Ryan hadn't looked at the body from that top angle. He chided himself for that. He always felt a step behind these days, like only half his brain was working. And the crabs had surprised him. He picked his way around the rocks in the little cove at the base of the niche, kneeled and used the gaff hook to push away some brownish-green kelp. The ranger was right. The skull had been hit, hard, compressed perhaps two inches in. Ryan did indeed have a likely homicide on his hands. And, Ryan thought, with a body that promised to be hard to identify. He sighed, almost groaned, in despair about getting stuck with an unidentified victim in an unsolvable case. What a great way to begin his time in Maine, he said to himself.

"No one liked him anyway," the ranger said, as if in consolation. "He was kind of a jerk."

Ryan looked up in surprise. He asked how the ranger knew that, given the lack of identifying features or documentation.

"Oh, that's Ricky Cutts," the ranger said. "Lobsterman out of Liberty Island."

Ryan looked at him in puzzlement.

"When I saw the buoy on the rope attached to the carcass, I noticed the number on it, 7135. I texted the state Department of Marine Resources and asked for the name of who held that license to fish for lobsters." He took out his cell phone to show Ryan the official response: "Commercial license: 7135. Holder: Ricky Cutts. Age: 35. Weight: 235. Height: 5 foot 9 inches. Eyes: Blue. Hair: Brown. Vessel: FV Pussy Man. Residence: 1 Alewife Road, Liberty Island, Maine." The matches were all there. Except for the blue eyes, of course. And where was the fishing vessel that was listed on that license?

Ryan looked at the ranger, hands held out flat and turned up, American body language for: *Dude, why didn't you tell me all this?*

"You didn't ask, J. Edgar," the ranger responded.

HEY BOSS

After the body of Ricky Cutts was delivered at the Liberty Island dock to the waiting ambulance, Ryan got into his truck. His exchanges with the park ranger had reminded him that he was not thinking at his best. He was forgetful and had been ever since the accident. He would walk into Hannaford's grocery store and not be able to remember what he had come to buy. He worried that his investigative powers were similarly impaired. He sat in the truck and stared at the yellow note he had taped to the dashboard: "Ask follow-up questions." It embarrassed him that he needed to remind himself of that elementary rule of investigation, things like, How do you know that? And, Who did you tell about this incident? Or, What do you think really happened? He had this unhappy feeling that he was basically a rookie again, starting all over, tripping over his own feet while onlookers chuckled and made snide comments to each other.

Then he drove north to his rented cottage on the outskirts of Bangor. The remoteness of the place struck him again. Maine was like no place he had ever lived or worked, having grown up in the suburbs of Orange County, California, back when it was still booming. As the miles went by, his mind drifted back to that increasingly distant time and place. After high school he felt a need to mature a bit, so he signed up for a three-year hitch in the navy, which trained him in basic engine work and assigned him to the minor-repairs section of the big service shipyard in San Diego. There he learned a lot about names of parts and tools but didn't see much of the world, except for three months of temporary duty on assignment to an air-conditioning unit on Guam, the most boring island in the Pacific. What can you say about an island whose national dish is Spam?

It developed that his navy job as an assistant engineman was to spend his days retrieving tools for someone who actually was allowed to use them, and then to clean up the mess after the job was done. His strongest memory was of being gruffly corrected several times a day by grizzled older sailors, as in "get the fucking five-inch grip, not the fucking five-inch clamp, you fucking moron." One thing he learned was that he didn't want to be an engine mechanic, so he left the navy to enroll at Cal Poly in San Luis Obispo, where he majored in criminal justice. In fact, he had met Marta in a sociology course they both took called Gender, Crime, and Violence. Then he went into law enforcement, she into teaching elementary school. They married, and a year later she had their first child.

As a newcomer at the FBI's field office in San Diego, he had been assigned to the health-care fraud team. Such investigations were not high-profile work, but they earned the bureau much credit, because finding the culprits helped save the federal government millions of dollars a day. The core of the work was investigating doctors who churned out Medicare bills that were either highly inflated or for nonexistent services. After a year of essentially working as an assistant, Ryan was tossed a small case on which, for the first time, he was the lead agent. It involved a doctor who exaggerated the workplace injuries of several dozen patients in exchange for a 25 percent cut of their insurance payments. Most of the necessary information was provided to him by insurance firms suspicious of the doctor's pattern of invoices. Ryan nailed the guy on wire fraud. The case involved total overpayments of about $200,000, penny-ante stuff compared to some of the big Medicare fraud cases. Normally it would have been too small to pursue, instead left to the insurance companies to recover their funds in civil suits, but Ryan's boss liked sending the signal to doctors that even small frauds made them vulnerable to criminal prosecution. Doctors didn't mind paying fines, but for some reason hated doing time, even when it was at the Club Fed up in Lompoc. And it was a good training wheels case for Ryan, making him do all the overview work like working with an assistant US attorney to prepare the charges and then writing a case summary.

Because his investigative work didn't involve imminent threats, his schedule was flexible, so he also was assigned a lot of liaison work with Customs, Border Patrol, and the DEA, even TSA. It was a job often given to a new guy, who was expendable, but it offered some valuable lessons about coordination, jurisdiction, and especially differing investigative techniques. The best agents, he decided after watching several different approaches, had a kind of dual mind: half coldly methodical, checking the boxes, but the other half imaginative and empathetic, ready to take leaps and filling in the steps later. For all that, he was embarrassed to say, he never had been the lead agent on a major investigation. The San Diego office simply was too well staffed for a newbie to be given the lead on anything that could make headlines, like going after violent bank robbers or Mexican narcotics cartels.

He turned off the pavement of the county highway and onto the mile-long dirt road that led to his rented house on a pond. In the wake of his family catastrophe, he was living on the other side of the continent, in the evergreen woods near a small, declining city that had peaked before the Industrial Revolution. Bangor had thrived in the first half of the nineteenth century, when the new American nation was hungry for the trees of Maine to burn for heat and to build ships and houses. In 1860 Bangor was the world's largest lumber port. But after the Civil War, the wood market collapsed as the nation shifted to oil and coal for warmth and to steel and brick for much of its construction material. The business of exporting Maine's thick winter crop of ice fell even harder with the rise of mechanical refrigeration. He had moved more than three thousand miles, but perhaps the time difference was greater than the distance. California had launched the postindustrial digital age; much of Maine had never made it all the way into the industrial age.

He did most of his paperwork at his kitchen table in his cottage, which sat on the shore of a small pond in the woods a few miles north of the city's airport. He only went to his FBI office in the chilly basement of the federal courthouse as needed. Anyway, that office was really just a cubbyhole, with no privacy. Customs, Border Patrol, coast guard, EPA, the Army National Guard, Social Security—they were the big federal dogs in Maine. The FBI in central and upper Maine was, well, him—one relatively young, badly rattled agent, unsure of where he was going in life. Even the Small Business Administration had a bigger presence in Maine than the bureau.

At home, he listened to a voicemail message on his cell phone from the Coast Guard's investigative service in Boston, which said the Guard's Rockfish station had passed along a report that a Maine-registered fishing boat had fetched up on the shoals west of Malpense Island. The Native Americans out there, the coast guard officer said, had hauled it off the rocks at high tide and then towed it into their nearby harbor. "Understand from Park Service that you are lead agent on inquiry related to boat," the clipped voicemail ended. He interpreted it as the bureaucratic equivalent of "tag, you're it." It was, he realized, the first voicemail or text he had received from someone outside the FBI since he had moved to Maine.

There's an old military saying he had heard in the navy: you want something bad enough, you'll get it bad enough. He had wanted isolation, and he had got it. On one of his first nights in the cottage, a still and windless evening, right after he moved in from the Motel 6, he had stood unmoving on the back porch. He had heard a low, almost inaudible "shush, shush," wondered where it came from—and realized it was his own blood, pushing through the carotid arteries on either side of his neck.

Ryan's predecessor as the FBI's man in Bangor had retired on the first day he was eligible for a full pension. He headed north, pulling a U-Haul to a log cabin on Scopan Lake, almost off the grid. It was way north in "the County," as Mainers called potato-rich Aroostook, Maine's northernmost and biggest county, almost a separate entity. The old guy had left behind an exceedingly thin Rolodex, and even what was there was sometimes outdated. In the bedraggled *M* section, Ryan found the entry for the cell phone number of the Malpense police chief in Southport. He left that man a message about his needing to go "examine a boat that wound up in your jurisdiction." He added, "Please consider it a federal crime scene."

His last call of the day was to check in with the boss—Harriet Williams, his supervisor in Portland. She was a natural manager—a low-key, by-the-book agent. She had gone from high school to the Naval Academy, served five years as a Marine Corps MP officer, and then gone to law school and the FBI. "Spent a lot of time in

Quantico," he observed to her, referring to the northern Virginia town that had both a major marine base and the FBI's training academy.

In their initial meeting, Harriet told Ryan she understood his desire to serve in Maine, given what had happened to his family. In fact, she said, she herself had requested her Portland assignment. At this point in her life, she said, she needed to slow down a bit. She had a husband who was an agent in the FBI's Boston office, and they had two small children at the house they had bought in New Hampshire, midway between Boston and Portland, with a reasonable commute to each. She wanted a few years at a quiet post in a good area to raise her children. After that, she would decide whether to punch out of federal employment and get into corporate security or a law practice oriented to financial crimes, or perhaps stay in the bureau and move up the hierarchy. She had her life organized in a rational way that Ryan once felt he had, but no longer. Now, for him, life was a matter of day-to-day, feeling fragmented much of the time. Making it through a week feeling fairly sane was as much as he dared ask.

He updated her on this new case that had fallen into his lap. She seemed pleased that it had come his way. "Good way to learn your territory," she said. Maine was an oddity when it came to crime. There were people behind bars in the state for stealing buckets of maple sap collecting in the woods for syrup makers. Others were doing time for stealing elvers, which were tiny glass eels in their juvenile state. Mainers didn't eat them, but people in China considered them a delicacy and were willing to pay $5,000 a pound for them. On the other hand, there hadn't been any serious bank robberies in Maine for two years, ones where the culprits remained at large for more than a day. Half the time, the tellers recognized the criminals and called their parents. And the Chinese intelligence agencies had far more productive places to spy on than Bangor, Augusta, or Portland. Ryan's purview also included public corruption, but Maine's politicians were perhaps the cleanest in the nation, with the worst known grift being the trips the head of the Turnpike Authority had taken to Europe, where he stayed in five-star hotels and dined lavishly. That was an accepted perk in other states. But in Maine, the jury, stirred by the prosecutor's argument that "it isn't what *we* do," found him guilty as hell, and the judge gave him a three-year stay in the state prison. Ryan also had noticed that internet fraud was his responsibility—in a state that was still tiptoeing into the digital age, with wide swaths that had neither cell phone coverage nor internet connections. So, Harriet had thought, the FBI's man in Bangor might as well follow this case down every hole. Ease him back in the game.

Harriet told him about something she'd learned early on in her time in Maine: that it was the only part of the United States traversed by the national railroad of another country. "True fact: the Canadian Pacific takes a shortcut from Quebec to New Brunswick, right across Maine." It is also, she noted, the only state with a one syllable name, which, she added, "has a certain logic to it, because it is the only state that borders only one other state."

Then, growing more serious, she asked a key question: "How are you doing? How is your personal life?"

"You mean, like, do I have any emotions?" he replied. He was parrying without really meaning to.

"I just need to know that you're moving in the right direction. You got hit with a pretty heavy dose of stress."

"Honestly," he said, "I'm going slow but okay."

"Are you eating well?"

"Not sure."

"That means you're not. You need to pay more attention to self-care."

Jesus, Harriet, he thought. But he knew she was right. He had been on the thin side all his life. Now, after five months of not really paying attention to food, he was skinny, standing six feet and an inch but weighing just 135. He once had been a man who looked well-built, well-balanced, even graceful, at home in the world. Now he did not. Shaving that morning, he had noticed that his jaw seemed to have tightened and stuck out more. He had become, he realized, a bit of a twitchy stick figure.

"Talk soon," she said. And that was quite enough managerial hand-holding for both of them.

He walked out on his cottage's small back deck. Lost Pond: too small for boating and attractive only to an occasional angler looking for bass, and when winter brought thick ice sometimes for skaters. There were only three other houses on the pond, and they all were uninsulated, summer-only "camps," as Mainers called them. So at this time of year, late May, he had the area to himself. He sipped an India pale ale made in Maine. The local craft beer scene had been a pleasant surprise to Ryan, who had grown up sipping Lagunitas in California. Since coming to Maine, he had pretty much been living on eggs, apples, and beer—not a balanced diet, he knew, but somehow its simplicity fit his estranged place in the world. Above the pines topping the low ridge across the pond, he saw the slow, heavenly lights of a big air force KC-10 tanker lining up to land at the Bangor airport.

And, he thought to himself, *for better or worse, you are now conducting an investigation.* He was back in the game. *I may be down,* he thought, *but I'm not out—in contrast to that body in the rocks, one Ricky Cutts.* He reviewed his case notes for the day, making some additions while the memories were fresh.

He hadn't gone running since before the accident, but now the urge hit him, probably because it had always helped him think about casework. He changed to shorts and sneakers and went out to jog the mile on the dirt road that went back out to the paved county road. About halfway along, a barred owl swooped him, close enough that Ryan could feel the breeze from the big bird's wings. Ryan was too big to be deemed prey, so the owl probably was just curious, or turf conscious, like so many other beings in Maine.

That night Ryan dreamed of San Diego, of the accident, of the blackness. It was exhausting, like climbing into a boxing ring every night and going several rounds against a masked heavyweight.

At 2:00 A.M. he finally conceded and got out of bed.

BREAKFAST ON LIBERTY ISLAND

He had never been to Liberty Island—he hadn't had a reason to do so during his short time in Maine. But it had been home to Ricky Cutts, the deceased lobsterman. Ryan drove through the deserted streets of Bangor at two thirty in the morning and headed south. It was a lovely drive through the woods along the east bank of the Penobscot River. He had never seen stars like this in California. He looked through the windshield up at the vivid splash of white curving across the middle of the sky and, for the first time in his life, grasped how the Milky Way had earned its name.

Then it was up the arch of the high green suspension bridge over Eggemoggin Reach, built in the 1930s, and onto Liberty Island. One of the more surprising aspects of the island that his predecessor had mentioned in his brief exit talk was that Liberty, like several remote parts of rural Maine, had no police force. "Locals don't want one," he said. If there was a serious crime, islanders could call the Hancock County sheriff's department. Often they did not make that call, he added with a shrug: "They say they like to handle their problems themselves." If the sheriff's three patrol cars all were busy, the dispatcher could tap the State

Patrol. In either event, when a law enforcement vehicle crossed the bridge and causeway, islanders went on alert and sent out calls of warning: "Staties on the island." It wasn't hostility to the police as much as a wariness of anyone from off island. And the customs there were indeed different, like driving with an open beer can in one's hand. One local joke was how driving distances were measured: "Castine? That's about three beers from here." Ryan wondered if his unknown FBI truck would receive the same skeptical welcome.

He arrived on the island at 4:00 A.M. At the first intersection, where the two paved side roads of the island met the main road to the harbor on the south coast of the island, he saw a convenience store named the Downeast Depot. It had a neon sign, blinking brightly in the predawn darkness, alternating between BEER in green and COFFEE in red. He went in and poured a cup of coffee into a Styrofoam cup. The drink was hot, but not even ample cream and sugar could disguise that it was both weak and burned, perhaps the worst he had encountered since his time in the navy. The greasy egg and cheese on a muffin was no better. He tried to eat this wretched breakfast standing at a small round table lacking chairs—no invitation to linger there. He used the moment to look over the place. Lobstermen, drowsily going through the morning routine, coming and going, getting coffee and an overpriced, underfilled submarine sandwich for their seagoing lunch. And for some, a six-pack of beer, for drinking aboard the boat after the day's hauling was done. They knew the prices as well as the clerk did. "That's thirteen forty-six," said the young man at the register. Even as he uttered it, the buyer dropped a crumpled ten and a five on the counter and left.

A handwritten sign over the counter advertised "lobster-y" rolls for twenty-four dollars. No one was buying those.

Ryan threw out the remaining half of the hapless muffin, got back in the truck, and drove down across Liberty. It was another seven miles to the south-facing harbor. There, cars and trucks were clustered outside a restaurant called the Fisherman's Pal. Inside, the restaurant was bustling, the air thick and humid with the rich, steamy aromas of brewing coffee, toasting bread, and sizzling bacon. Ryan surveyed the place, partly out of lawman's habit. Most of the tables were full, even at four thirty in the morning. These were working people in the northeasternmost part of the nation. Their labors began at dawn and lasted until about midafternoon. That was partly because the mornings were less windy out on the ocean, making it easier to fish then. But it was also because in the depths of winter, this far east and north, the sky grew light around six o'clock in the morning and dark by four o'clock in the afternoon. That solar cycle also set the work schedule for the boat-yard, the biggest single employer in town.

Even though the restaurant was crowded, five vacant stools stood at the end of the counter. Ryan slid onto the red plastic of the leftmost. A red-haired waitress glared at him but otherwise did not acknowledge him. He waited. Read the menu. Waited more. Bits of conversation floated across the room, particularly from the corners, which acted as amplifiers.

"Hey, your new impeller came in."

"Thanks, I'll stop by."

"Ain't cheap."

"Never is."

It had the feel of a town conversing with itself, of one big exchange among lifelong familiars. A man came in and stopped by a table. "Sorry to hear about your mother. She doing better?"

Ryan heard another quick exchange: "Bought that new floating rope, I think it parts too easily."

The person next to him said, "Goddam federal regulations. Fuck the whales."

Another guy walked in the front door and saw someone eating breakfast in one of the booths. The one just arriving shouted across the room, "Hey, numbnuts, your truck is blocking mine on the wharf."

"Sorry, Bill, I thought you was still down in Portland." He held a forkful of scrambled eggs in front of his mouth.

"You know I had to be back for the selectman's meeting."

"Was that last night? I forgot. How'd it go?" The fork hovered.

"Well, we've got to increase some property taxes to pay for the snowplowing and road salt this coming winter. And right now, I'm feeling like we should raise yours."

"Fuck you too." Laughs on both sides. Hearty, good-natured Maine banter. The forkful of egg finally concluded its journey.

The first man offered a solution. "Look, you need to block someone, park in front of Ricky Cutts's old truck. I hear he ain't gonna be using it for a while." A couple of faces turned to look at the speaker.

That exchange also caught Ryan's ear. While he pondered it, he tried again to signal the waitress. She snorted and kept going. Ryan couldn't understand the situation. What had he done wrong? She passed by him a third time.

Eventually a man in healthy middle age, perhaps forty-five or fifty, settled down on the stool to Ryan's right. "Helen, would you please give this poor guy a cup of coffee?" he cajoled in a voice that was at once half-exasperated yet also expressed gratitude to the waitress for protecting his territory.

He reached his right hand over to Ryan. It was callused and cracked, with a few prominent white scars. Even seasoned fishermen got slashed by lobsters sometimes. "I'm Caleb Goodwin," he said with a straightforward, friendly tone. A black shock of hair hung over his forehead. His eyes were blue and steady. His chin was square but unshaven, with a bit of gray in the stubble, but he still projected an air of vigor, a man willing and eager to take on what this world would throw at him each day. And today it had fetched up this fellow from the federal government.

Helen poured Ryan a cup of coffee but did not look at him. "He took your stool, Caleb," she said quietly to the man on Ryan's right.

"Chrissake, Helen, give him a break. He's from the government. He's FBI."

Ryan was surprised Caleb knew that. Three other men walked in together and took the remaining counter stools. Helen knew all their regular orders. "Helen's just trying to look out for us," Caleb said to Ryan, in half apology for the waitress's rudeness. "We're the Highliners, we meet here at this counter every Thursday morning." He waved a hand toward the three men to his right. "Herc, Tim, and Guppy." They nodded at Ryan, a stiff Maine hello. To Ryan's eye, the three looked like members of an aging country-rock band, except that they had a formality to them, at least with outsiders. This was unfamiliar to Ryan, who had grown up with the easy ways of suburban Southern California, where most people in a neighborhood were relative newcomers. There, everyone was from somewhere else. Here, everyone was from right damn here, often for a couple of centuries. Sometimes their surnames were the same as local landforms—harbors, peninsulas, islands.

The mouth of the last Highliner hung open a bit, which Ryan guessed was the cause of the unusual nickname. They were all middle-aged, sharing the air of successful, independent working men who answered only to themselves and their peers. All wore cotton shirts, work pants, and baseball caps. One cap featured the logo of the Red Sox baseball team, another the Cummins engine company, and the third, on Guppy, was decorated in the feathery dark greens and browns of hunting camouflage.

"Social club?"

"Yes and no," Caleb said. "Mainly, we're guys who have fished here for a long time and are good at it." Once a week they breakfasted together, Caleb explained. Most other mornings, he said, they held a brief huddle on the wharf before separating to drive their boats out to their individual fishing grounds. That quick meeting would review any weather issues. Foremost, they would consider whether it was too rough to fish that day. The custom was that if they decided not to go, no one else would. "I dunno how that started, but it's always been that way, even back when my grandfather was a Highliner." At their weekly breakfasts they'd review the state of the business: What were the middlemen offering at the dock for landed lobster per pound? What direction was the price of fuel going? And the cost of bait? Those were the three key financial variables in the trade. Their directions could make the difference between a season of bounty or catastrophe.

There were also more personal issues to review. Perhaps a town fisherman was aging, maybe needed some help hauling; maybe suggest hiring a teenager as a sternman, and teach him the business. Or is a newbie aggressively placing his traps perhaps a mite close to the customary grounds of another fisherman?

Ryan asked how one became a member of the Highliners. "You don't, really," Caleb said. "You get told that you are. You have to be one of the most productive fishermen, doing well for several years, and you have to have some judgement, which frankly a lot of fellows don't." He said that Guppy was the newest one. "It was seven years ago that we invited him to take a stool at our breakfast." At the end of the line of stools, Guppy raised his hunting cap in acknowledgment.

"And yourself?" Ryan asked.

"Feels like forever," Caleb said.

Herc, at Caleb's right, piped up. "He's too modest to tell you. Youngest Highliner ever, selected when he was just twenty-five. Just a pup, but already recognized then as one of the most consistent fishermen and also a dependable guy."

The coffee at the Fisherman's Pal was richer than the thin, bitter stuff back at the Downeast Depot. Ryan took a gulp and then asked how Caleb had known who he was. "No big mystery," Caleb said. "The lobstering community lives on the CB radio, usually channel sixteen. You're out there alone, or with one helper, so you monitor it while working, trading news of the day: Why wasn't so-and-so's boat out? Was he at the Sox game, or had a child graduating from high school? Didn't you hear, his mother was taken to hospital over to Ellsworth? Oh, that's a shame, she was my second and third grade teacher, back when those classes were combined." In summary, he said, "Lotsa chitchat."

So yesterday afternoon, he explained, many had overheard the transmission from the skipper of the Isle au Haut ferry.

"What did he say?" Ryan asked.

"He was bellyaching, telling his office that he was gonna be 'fifteen fucking minutes late 'cause there's a goddamn government man wants a dead body picked up down to Duck Harbor way.' That comment set the radio sets chattering." Caleb and the others had moved over to channel ninety-six, which was more private but hardly confidential.

"You notice things," Caleb said. "Just now, I was walking from the commercial wharf over to the Fisherman's Pal for the Highliners' weekly breakfast. I saw a white four-wheel drive Ford F-150 pickup parked out front. Didn't recognize it," he said. "Then I had noticed the white GS license plates, so I knew it belonged to the federal government. I also noticed it had a funny-looking antenna, ending with a kind of black can, which I'd only seen on some law enforcement vehicles." Ryan did not say anything, but that was part of the truck's setup to receive bursts of encrypted communications while he was in the truck. "I walked in, saw you, and thought, here's a from-away. He's dressed too neat to be a tourist, wearing black shoes, and he doesn't know the counter rules. Okay, so I think to myself, that's his pickup outside, and he's probably the ferry skipper's 'government man.'" It was simple addition for someone well attuned to the vibes of the island.

Ryan was intrigued by this lobsterman's sleuthing. "How did you know I wasn't DEA?" he asked, referring to the Drug Enforcement Administration.

Caleb looked over the lip of his coffee cup and dryly replied, "Probably not drive around with GS plates, you know?"

"Or NOAA?" Ryan persisted, referring to the National Oceanic and Atmospheric Administration, whose mission included regulating the fisheries.

"Last time I looked, they didn't wear ankle holsters," Caleb observed, with a quick glance downward at Ryan's service-issue Glock 19M, just above the right shoe.

"I'm impressed," Ryan confessed, hoping he wasn't blushing, and suppressing the urge to tug down his pants leg. He nodded. Message received: don't underestimate these islanders.

Caleb had a way of pausing before speaking, as if reviewing his thought before offering it. He was someone who knew his words carried weight in his world. Sometimes they would be repeated around the island, passed along almost as rulings that had the impact of law, or at least tradition. The line between those two things was hazy on Liberty Island.

At about 5:00 A.M., the front door of the café burst open. Two young women, teenaged sisters by their appearance, burst through the door. They were laughing, but more out of nervous energy than at anything amusing. Ryan looked and thought they were drunk or high, or both. Maybe panicky. Other people in the café were beginning their days, but the girls clearly were near the end of a very long night of partying.

They were wearing black plastic coats that were supposed to look like leather but really did not. Both looked emaciated. The taller one, who had dyed blonde hair with the bangs colored pink, wore a jacket whose front featured studs that were supposed to look like steel, but really just looked like plastic painted with chrome colors. The shorter one, perhaps fifteen years old, had colored her long hair entirely purple. She had some yellow and blue blotches on her neck that could be bruises or could be makeup—it was hard to tell. Her black eye mascara had streaked down onto her cheeks, because she had been crying earlier and had wiped her face without a mirror. The black streaks were the most real aspect of her visage. The purpose of their punk look was to grab the viewer's attention and say, "Hey, look at me." But in reality the appearance of the two girls was sad and made people avert their eyes after a moment.

The girls slipped into the two chairs of the small table by the front window. The waitress grimaced but still went over to offer them coffee from the pot she carried. "Fuck that shit," the pinkish one said, almost shouting, and waving a hand in the air. "We want beer." Their night was not quite over.

Helen had been through this before. "No beer until lunchtime," she reminded them, "and that begins at ten thirty."

"Okay, fuck it, just bring us onion rings and Cokes," the purple one said loudly.

Several people glanced over at the girls, but not with alarm or surprise. "Everyone here knows them," Caleb explained softly. "Ricky Cutts's daughters, Teena and Marie. Wild family. People give them some slack because they've been through a lot."

One thing Ryan thought he could do well was maintain a poker face. But Caleb seemed to pick up some vibe, perhaps a quickening in Ryan's posture or a flicker of interest in his eyes. "Oh. What do you know about him?" the lobsterman asked.

"I'd never heard his name until yesterday," Ryan said honestly. "And then?"

Ryan leaned in closer, putting his head near Caleb's. "Who around here would want to kill Ricky Cutts?" he asked earnestly.

Caleb grinned broadly and opened up his hands as if that were about the funniest thing he had heard in weeks. He leaned back, looked around the café, crowded at 5:00 A.M. with lobstermen and workers from the boatyard. Then he said, almost booming, "Hell, who wouldn't?" The other Highliners nodded: *you got that right.* The feeling of local folk wisdom hung in the warm air.

There had been no official announcement, but they all seemed to know Cutts was dead, Ryan realized. He must have stiffened with suspicion.

"Relax. It's the same as knowing you're an FBI man," Caleb Goodwin said. "Basic addition." Body found, washed up on Isle au Haut. There had been a lot of radio talk yesterday, he said. "Any lobstermen missing lately?" "Yep, Ricky Cutts, his fishing ground is down below there, haven't seen his boat on his mooring for at least two days, and that twenty-year-old beat-up silver Toyota Tundra of his has been parked at the end of the commercial wharf for the last two days and nights. And who in Japan thought that 'Tundra' was a good name for a truck? Not someone who had ever been up there." Likely conclusion: "What do you think?" "Good chance it's old Ricky." No one in the radio chatter had expressed much surprise. Or regret.

The two girls finished their snack and left as noisily as they had entered, letting the screen door slam with a bang and laughing too much about too little. "Later, losers!" one yelled—another message that was the opposite of what it intended to say. These were girls who already at their young ages had come up short in life's lottery.

Ryan told Caleb he'd need to interview those two.

"Not hard to find, or hear, as you just saw," Caleb said. "Either here, or at the Fogged Inn bar, or on the wharf smoking. Or, lately, at the women's shelter." *Or*, he thought, *scratching around for meth or coke or grass*, but he didn't say that out loud.

"But not at Ricky Cutts's house?"

"No," Caleb said. "Last I heard, both were sleeping at Sarah's Shelter." He pointed upward to his left. "Up the hill," he said. "Little brown house at the top on the right."

Ryan asked if there was a wife. "There was," Caleb said. "Wanda. She's been gone, what, at least ten years or so."

Herc, two seats down, added that, "One night she run out of Ricky's house with a split lip and a black eye, and was never seen on the island again. Heard she went back to her hometown, Baltimore." Ryan thanked Caleb and Herc for their help, left three one-dollar bills on the counter for his coffee, and stood.

It was still early, so before trying the shelter, Ryan drove northeastward on the island to Ricky Cutts's house, the only building actually on Alewife Road. The yard was itself a safety hazard, strewn with half-deconstructed old outboard engines, barnacled buoys, rusted winches, tangles of fishing rope, a big drinks cooler missing a lid, and other cast-off gear from the fishing trade. Rolls of chicken wire. A shovel without a handle. Two old, cracking truck tires. The front end of a 1950s Plymouth pickup truck. Five-gallon yellow-and-white plastic buckets, useful for carrying fish, sand, or water. A child's big sit-in toy car, yellow and orange. Those things are indestructible, Ryan thought to himself. The yard mess hardly made Cutts's place unusual. In Maine it was considered a sin to throw out anything that might actually prove useful one day. Old engine blocks, for example, make fine anchors for mooring buoys, sinking slowly into bottom mud and holding their ground even through a blowy winter storm.

Watching his step, Ryan picked his way to the front door. The house itself was one story, with tar paper siding nailed over the original wooden shingles, and a brick chimney in serious need of repointing. Ryan knocked on the door, waited, knocked again, and then tried the doorknob. It was, to his surprise, unlocked.

Ryan shouted hello and then inspected the living room—beer cans, pornographic magazines, and empty potato chip bags. The kitchen was no better. Mouse droppings dotted the linoleum floor and the two cupboards, where the rodents had chewed into boxes of instant macaroni and cheese. Some cans of sardines. Nothing much in the refrigerator but curdling milk, beer, and American cheese.

"Hello," Ryan yelled up the narrow staircase and then ascended it. There were two bedrooms upstairs, but only one looked like it had been used lately. In the bigger one, men's clothes were thrown into a corner. The other bedroom was empty, with two small frames supporting bare mattresses. Above the farther bed, spray-painted in black on the bare wall, were the words, in foot-tall letters, "I HATE YOU ILL TELL". The sole bathroom, at the top of the stairs between the two rooms, was downright filthy, with yellow scum dried on the porcelain sink. There were just four things on the sink: a frazzled toothbrush, a comb, a bar of white soap with oil in its cracks, and a T-shirt that had been used as a towel. No toothpaste, Ryan noticed.

Out front again, he went over to the mailbox and opened it. It was stuffed full of shoppers, junk mail, and, he noticed, a letter from the island's high school sent in late February. None of it had been opened.

He went back and sat on the front steps and thought for a while, just trying to absorb the spirit of Ricky Cutts. Yet he felt no such stirring, just a sense that Cutts had led a difficult, malignant, and wasteful life.

He drove back to town and parked near the bank, at the eastern end of Main Street. He walked westward, studying the place in the clear morning sunlight. At its eastern end, just past the bank, stood one of the town's two lobster co-ops. This co-op extended credit to lobstermen in exchange for them selling exclusively to it, and so here they made their daily purchases of fuel and bait. Next stood the town's sole bar, the Fogged Inn, which, by policy stated on the wall, did not extend credit to anyone. Near it stood the short wharf that belonged to the Isle au Haut ferry, which ran the forty-minute trip out to that island in all but the most extreme weather. Next, just to the west, was the town library—an essential service, because many Mainers got through the five months of winter by reading books or watching DVDs of lengthy miniseries.

Across the street lay the "yacht wharf," the smaller of the two piers extending into the harbor. Maine Street then ran past some froufrou shops, attractive to tourists who didn't know what to do with themselves once they arrived. These stores made a fortune selling sweatshirts when the July fogs rolled in off the Gulf of Maine and pulled the daytime temperature down into the fifties. Then there was the Fishermen's Pal and, next to it, the town office. Farther to the west was the big commercial wharf, with its eighty parking spots reserved for the vehicles of those working in the lobster industry. Next on the harbor was the other lobster co-op. Finally, at the western end of Main Street, was the boatyard, the island's single largest employer, its docks filled with fishing boats, sailboats, power boats, and even an aging ferryboat that needed a rebuild.

It took Ryan about thirty minutes to walk the entire span of Maine Street from one co-op to the other. At every step there were lovely views with lobster boats and yachts in the foreground and an archipelago of some forty-five green islands in the background, dominated in the distance by the long south-running ridge of Isle au Haut—"the high island," seventeenth-century French mariners had dubbed it, because they could see it from well out to sea.

Walking back, Ryan noticed how Main Street was level, running between the harbor and the base of the hill on which the town's houses perched. That hill essentially was a huge mass of granite with a thin layer of dirt atop it. For most of its history, the town's raw sewage slid through pipes laid atop the soil and into the harbor, where the tide would eventually bury it or carry it away. This system had the unintended side effect of helping preserve Port Liberty from tourism, because on hot summer days the piles of sewage baking on the mudflats at low tide exuded a powerful odor. Then, in the 1990s, the federal Environmental Protection Agency informed the town that it must devise a more sanitary way to deal with its effluence. With the aid of a multimillion-dollar federal grant, workmen spent over a year blasting channels through the living granite and laying in place a system of pipes and pumps. Suddenly, without a harbor dotted with steaming feces, the town found itself deemed quaint and charming. Nowadays it had a winter population of three thousand, but that tripled from mid-June through Labor Day.

SARAH'S SHELTER

It was still relatively early, just past eight, when Ryan knocked on the front door of the small shelter for women. He had learned that the work day began early in Maine. There was no sign out front, but Caleb's directions had been clear, and there was only one brown house on the right side of the road at the top of the hill. Its front entrance confirmed that he was at the right place. It had the telltale bruised look of an entrance to a shelter for abused women. This was a door that, more than once, someone had stood outside of, shouting and kicking in a blind rage. A steel plate had been riveted across the bottom third. He glanced left and right and saw that the windows on either side were covered inside by steel mesh. He knocked three times. Waited. Knocked again three times.

He heard one bolt lock turn. Then another. The door opened a few inches, still held by two separate chains. Between the chains, he could see the left side of a woman's face, and, on her right hip, consciously turned away from him, a holstered .22 Ruger pistol. The perfect weapon, he thought, for the job of waving off unwanted visitors without bringing too much firepower to the job. "No men," she said softly, shaking her head as she spoke.

"I'm FBI."

"You heard me," she said, looking up at him and speaking more loudly, and not giving him an inch. This was a woman who had had enough, he sensed, and probably had been trained in how to draw uncrossable lines. "Not about you. About women and girls here."

"I have questions," he said.

"Please take your questions to Mister Buck." It turned out that an islander named Absalom Buck was the chairman of the board of directors of Sarah's Shelter. And pretty much its major financial supporter, making sure the place kept going with enough heating oil to keep its furnace running all winter. She handed him a business card that had Buck's name and number on it and began to close the door, then opened it slightly again.

"You said you're FBI?" she asked.

"Yes," he said. "Out of Bangor."

"You ever need help, you can call me, okay?" she said, her voice low. "My cell is below Abby's on the card."

Ryan was puzzled. Was her response intended to be sympathetic, like even the women's shelter was in on the gag about Ryan being the FBI loser in Bangor? He didn't see a woman's name on the card. "Are you Sarah?"

"Nah, I'm Louise." She closed the door. Ryan heard the locks turning conclusively.

Walking back to his truck, he wondered if instead Louise had been trying to tell him something. He had learned as an agent to listen to that little second-guessing voice in the back of his head, the one that said, *Maybe you are missing something here.* But what? He admired her cautious toughness. She struck him as a fellow survivor.

He needed to know more about the turbulent Cutts family. He decided to stop by the high school.

SCHOOL DAY

The security guard at the front door was awed by the FBI badge and personally escorted Ryan directly past the secretary and into Principal Wheatley's office. There was a chair on either side of the desk and a small sofa on the side of the room. The principal, one of those vaguely appearing pale men who could be anywhere between forty and sixty, was wearing a gray sweater and black slacks. The outfit only served to underscore his graying hair and sagging face.

Ryan handed him his FBI business card and said he was looking into a situation with Ricky Cutts, an island resident. "His children attend school here," Ryan said.

The principal, sitting behind his desk, nodded wearily. Yet, after an initial back and forth, plus a bit of hemming and hawing, he proved disinclined to say anything much at all. "Privacy laws and such," he said apologetically. "You know I'd like to help you, but . . . ," he said. He waved his hands upward and stood. *Discussion over*, his body language meant. *Nothing I can do.*

Across the desk, Ryan remained seated. He leaned back in his chair and closed his eyes.

The principal waited. And waited. Finally, after a full minute, he said, "Uh, Mr. Tapia, what are you doing?"

"Imagining," Ryan said softly.

"Imagining what?" Wheatley said.

"The headline in the newspaper: 'Liberty Principal Refuses to Help FBI Inquiry.' Type of headline that could live on the internet for years, you know?" Ryan was impressed with himself. He usually couldn't bring himself to apply this sort of pressure, but the principal's dismissive manner had provoked him. He opened his eyes: "I just want to talk to their teachers, female teachers, if they had any."

The principal caved instantly. His eyes flashed: this FBI man might know more than he was letting on. The Cutts girls, he knew off the top of his head, had two female teachers, he said. One taught history and had the older Cutts girl, Teena, in the eleventh grade homeroom. The other taught English and had the younger one, Marie, in the ninth grade homeroom. "They're sisters, the two teachers," Wheatley said. "Twins, in fact."

He returned with the two teachers in two minutes. They were identical twins, and in fact were dressed in matching blue jeans and Red Sox sweatshirts. Both had pointy noses, small bright blue eyes, and black hair pulled back in ponytails. To Ryan's eye, they looked like high school students themselves.

"We're the Fitches. We're from Dover," said the one on the left. She said they had graduated from the University of New Hampshire the previous June and had wanted to teach together, but for months were unable to find posts that fit. "We wanted to work together. We were worried we were going to have to be apart," she said. "Then, in August, the two slots here at Liberty High opened up. We jumped at it."

"And the Cutts girls?" Ryan asked, trying to move along this personal history.

She bobbed her head, eager to please. "So in mid-January," she said, "it's about 4:00 P.M., after school. I'm sitting in my classroom correcting tests. It was, 'The Gilded Age: Railroads, Industry, and Westward Expansion.' It's getting dark outside. Suddenly the lights go out. I thought it was a power outage, but then a hand grabs my ponytail, and I can sense this guy behind me—smells, I don't know, sour? Like anger, sweat, and diesel fumes."

"What happened next?" Ryan said.

"He jerked my head back a little and said, 'Have you been talking to my Marie?' I said, 'Marie who?' and he said, 'Marie Cutts.'" The teacher began to cry. "I was stupid," she continued, "and I said, 'No, I have Teena, and she hasn't come to school since before Christmas.' He dropped my hair and left."

The history teacher stopped for a minute, unable to continue. "I was hyperventilating, so scared I sat there shaking and peed myself. I was grabbing some tissues, dabbing it up, wiping the chair, and then I realized, oh no. I ran out and down the hall." She stopped.

Neither of the young women spoke.

"And?" Ryan asked, finally.

Now the one on the left was almost shouting as the memory came back. "And I got to my sister's classroom and flipped on the light, and she was sitting there at her desk, blood running from her nose all down her chin and front. She was sobbing. So was I."

Ryan looked at the twin on the right. "And?"

The English teacher said, "My own classroom had gone dark. Next thing I knew, a hand on the back of my head slammed my face into my desk. All he said was, 'Stop talking to Marie.' And he walked out. That was it."

The two had cleaned themselves up in the girls' room, then headed to the principal's office.

"And?" Ryan said.

The twin teachers swiveled to look at Principal Wheatley. He was sitting with his forehead held in both his hands, propped on the desk. "I told them," he said slowly, with evident unhappiness, "that the school couldn't afford to go to war with the community."

"Which meant?" Ryan said.

"Which meant, drop it," Wheatley said in the same monotone.

"And that was it?" Ryan said, looking back to the girls.

"Pretty much," said "History" Fitch. She related that they had walked out together to the little red Kia in which they commuted, only to find the windshield smashed in. They pushed the shards out of the way and started to drive, then realized that all four wheels were flat, having been punctured with a knife or ice pick. "We called Plato down at the Irving station. He said he was closed, but after he heard us crying, he came up in the tow truck anyway, hooked up the Kia, gave us a ride home. We took the bus to school the next morning, and he dropped off the car at school, with a new windshield and tires. Also changed the oil and filters. Wouldn't let us pay, said it was his PTA contribution."

Ryan asked "English" Fitch if Marie had ever told her much about her home life. "Not really," the young woman said. "All I really knew was she was an unhappy girl." The first time they talked was when she didn't want to leave after school was over, and kept saying, "Life sucks." The second time that happened, she asked the teacher if it was her own fault when bad things happened. "She cried some," the teacher said. "I didn't know what to say. I told her she needed to talk to a counselor. That's what I think set him off." But after Ricky Cutts had visited the school, the teacher said, Marie would not talk at all. "In about mid-February," she added, "Marie also stopped coming to school."

"Anything else?" Ryan asked.

"We're leaving this school after graduation in a few weeks," "English" Fitch added. "Gonna sub down in Portland. Maybe go to law school."

At this, Principal Wheatley spoke up again. "I'm so sorry, girls."

Ryan looked at the scene. *The young have more resilience than the old*, he thought. This man was worn down and used up. People can only take so much. He wondered how many times people like Ricky Cutts had confronted the principal through the years, how many mornings the man had looked up to see an angry parent shouting, "Don't you dare!" And how many times he had wondered if that maddened adult was carrying a pistol or had left one around the house that a deranged child might bring to school one day.

"I'm moving too, to the junior high in Gorland," the principal said. He added that he had banned Ricky Cutts from the school for one year and sent him a letter informing him of that action. That explained the unopened letter in the mailbox, Ryan thought.

"Well, good for you," Ryan said. He turned back to the Fitches. "I wish you women good luck. My own wife was a teacher, and I know it can be hard." The two teachers left the office.

Wheatley sighed. He felt like everyone in the world was angry with him, including this FBI man who just appeared from nowhere to add to the misery.

Ryan stood. As he placed his hand on the office doorknob, he turned. "I'm sorry I pushed you," he said to the principal.

Silent tears were rolling down the man's cheeks. He looked up, surprised that Ryan was still present. "That's the job," he said in the same resigned monotone. Ryan wasn't sure whether the principal was talking about Ryan's job or his own. Maybe both.

ABBY BUCK, ISLAND ENTREPRENEUR

From the truck's cab, Ryan called Absalom Buck, the leading financial backer for Sarah's Shelter, who agreed to meet Ryan for coffee in fifteen minutes "down at the Pal." Ryan drove back to the waterfront, parked, walked into the restaurant, and found an open booth. Before sitting he looked across the dining room to Helen for approval of his seat selection. She nodded. He sat. The room was far emptier now. It was the midmorning lull, with the breakfasters all long gone to work. The lunch crowd wouldn't begin trickling in until about 10:45 A.M.

Buck appeared, a thirtyish-year-old man. He was dressed not like a fisherman but perhaps a prosperous island businessperson, in trim new blue jeans, a tan L.L. Bean corduroy shirt, and a jacket made of real black leather. He was careful but open to questions. "Call me Abby," he said, extending his hand.

"What do you know about Ricky Cutts?" Ryan asked.

"Not much. We run in different circles," Buck said. "He's a fisherman; I'm an entrepreneur." He explained what he meant by that. "Since I was a teenager, I had this ability to notice where there was a good profit margin to be had. After my freshman year of high school, I started selling ice cream from a little stand on the side of the main street, next to the library. Made a run one night a week to buy the ice cream and cones, worked there all day, seven days a week. I made several thousand dollars three summers in a row. By the time I graduated from high school, I had enough money to open a store, up at the top of the island."

Buck waited while Helen placed two coffees on the table. "Hey, Abby, thanks for the donation for the school trip," she said.

"Happy to help," Buck responded. He looked back to Ryan. "What I had was the willingness to provide what was needed. On this island, that basically means providing essentials at odd hours—before dawn, around midnight."

"For example?" Ryan asked.

"You saw the Downeast Depot store?" Buck asked.

"Stopped there this morning," Ryan said.

"That's mine," Buck said. "I got three of them, one on each bridged island. Beer and whiskey at 1:00 A.M. for the drinkers, and then three hours later, coffee and breakfast sandwiches for the fishermen—and sometimes they're the same guys. You can charge a lot for that around here. And 'lobster-y rolls' for the tourists; they eat them up."

"Why just for the tourists?"

"My rolls aren't for Mainers." He leaned forward and said, in a lowered voice, that he would let Ryan in on a business secret: "It's just Costco crabmeat from Indonesia, mixed with celery and Costco mayo, served in a Costco hot dog bun brushed with melted butter from Costco. With three little pieces of lobster claw meat dropped on top. Doesn't taste bad. Costs me maybe four bucks a roll. During the summer we sell twenty or thirty a day. People arrive hungry and want a taste of the real Maine. And they want it served by someone who talks like a Mainer. We provide that, uh, 'authentic experience.' But Mainers know better. They tend to eat lobster at home, or maybe on a night on the town. But not in convenience stores."

Ryan considered that margin. Gross profit of twenty dollars each, say thirty a day, seven days a week. More than three thousand dollars a week, just on the phony lobster rolls.

Buck watched him. "*A-yuh*, we're just simple folk of the coast," he said, using an exaggerated version of the Maine affirmative. Then he dropped the put-on Down East accent. "Pays a lot of the bills."

Helen walked by, opened a side door, sat down on the granite steps outside with a loud sigh, and savored a cigarette. Midway through it, she yelled over her shoulder to the man at the cash register, with a weariness in her voice, "Charlie, you really need to get that busboy hired." The man nodded.

Ryan felt he had a sense of who Abby Buck was. Time to move along. He said, "Who is Sarah?"

"As in the shelter?" Buck asked.

Ryan nodded.

"She was my mother," Buck said quickly. "Gone now." He cast his eyes down at the table. He didn't want to discuss how, when he was a boy, his father had more or less beaten her to death, knowing she had nowhere to go after her own family had kicked her out for getting pregnant while an unmarried teenager. When Louise was starting the shelter, he had gone to offer support and had told her the story of his mother, and Louise had said in turn that she wanted to name it in honor of her. It would give other women the refuge Sarah had desperately needed and couldn't find. When he finished relating this, Buck sat silently, still staring downward at his coffee.

"I'm sorry," Ryan said. He waited politely, then switched to the topic that really interested him: "Who killed Ricky Cutts?"

Buck looked up quickly. "So it's official?"

"Pretty much," Ryan said.

Buck sighed and shook his head. He took a moment to assess the departure of Ricky Cutts, then said, "Well, then this world is a better place."

"Oh?" Ryan said. He found that response provocative. It might be true, but why say it?

"Ricky caused a lot of trouble over the years," Buck said. But, he continued, the thing that really caused the break with Cutts's own relatives wasn't his lawbreaking, but when he had sold the waterfront land he owned without telling them. "They found that unforgivable and said so pretty loudly, all around town."

"Was it their land too?" Ryan asked.

"Not legally," Buck said, "but it had been in their family since the Revolution. Their ancestor had been a soldier, got it as a veteran's land grant after the war." Buck added that it was on a valued stretch of "bold coast," meaning it had deep water so one could moor a boat just a short way offshore and it wouldn't ground with every low tide, which was not good for the hull or for the paint on the bottom. "They were pissed." To make it worse, he said, he didn't sell the land to an islander, but to a retired CIA guy who didn't talk to anyone, didn't participate in any activities or even contribute to charities, as was expected of deep-pocketed summer people. "Real standoffish prick. Built a house down there on the water, put in a wharf."

Buck got up to leave. "Gotta check my stores," he said.

Ryan took some notes, then went to his truck. He was wondering about Buck. Clearly Buck knew more about Cutts than he let on. Buck had known that something had happened to Cutts, and he was not unhappy about that news. Were people on this island going to line up and volunteer to be suspects?

A LOBSTERMAN'S WAKE

O fficial confirmation of the demise of Ricky Cutts came with the harbormaster posting a notice on the fishing wharf's bulletin board, as was the custom. The fishing community came together, as always. There would not be regular trap hauling that day. Instead, they followed the usual practice for a fallen fisherman. The town's entire working fleet—one of the largest in Maine, with perhaps eighty-five boats in all, including a dozen older, semiretired men who went out just two or three days a week—gathered and headed down in their various boats to Ricky's fishing ground. Each pulled a stack of Ricky's traps and brought them back to the Liberty commercial wharf, where they would load them into their trucks and deliver them to his house on Alewife Cove. Tim, one of the Highliners, was collecting the lobsters from Cutts's traps and would deliver them to the co-op and then leave "the cash-out money" at the shelter for Cutts's daughters, even though they'd probably spend it all on alcohol and other mind-altering substances. That was their own business, islanders believed.

Ryan was standing on the wharf watching the fleet come in, two or three of the high-bowed, low-sterned boats every few minutes, some sending up rooster tail wakes. Caleb appeared at his shoulder.

"Fine sight," he said. He had not participated in collecting Ricky's traps.

"You're not going to the house?" Ryan asked.

"No," Caleb shook his head. "Wouldn't be right. We weren't close."

There was something off in that response, Ryan thought. Even if a man was not liked, isn't that what you did around here?

Caleb looked at him and seemed to sense his thought. "There's a lot you don't understand about Liberty. And a lot I can't say in the Pal. Come out with me tomorrow. You need to know these waters, how they work. And we can talk on the boat."

Ryan accepted the invitation.

At Ricky's house, as is also traditional, the island's lobstering community held an informal fisherman's wake. After heaping Ricky's traps in the backyard, they grilled burgers and sausages and drank beer and spent the afternoon telling wild stories about their departed comrade of the sea. Cutts's two girls were nowhere to be seen, which was neither surprising nor bothersome. They had not been invited, one of the Highliners, Herc, had said when one of the others asked him, because they did not need to hear those old tales. Many of them ended with, "And Ricky was so drunk that . . . ." Ricky had not led an exemplary life. He had been gaff-hooked out of the water more than once before that final time on Isle au Haut.

Back in his truck, Ryan checked his voicemails, texts, and emails. The lawyer representing his family in the civil suits stemming from the accident reported that the truck driver had declared bankruptcy, and the construction firm was likely to follow soon. "That leaves their insurance company as the target," the lawyer's message said. "Call me." Ryan didn't care.

He went to the next message, which was from a man in Quoddy Island, Maine, up near the Canadian border. The man said, with some humor, that he had retired as Malpense tribal police chief a full three years ago. "You federal guys might wanna update your Rolodex, or check the internet," he chided. At any rate, he added, Ryan would need to call not the tribal police chief, but Johnny Mac, the police officer for the southern branch of the Malpense tribe. "That's his turf; he's the subchief down there," he reported. It wasn't clear to Ryan whether that subchief position was a tribal rank or a police post—or if the distinction even mattered.

That night, Ryan had another accident dream. This time Marta and the kids were locked on the other side of a wall. A flood was coming, but he couldn't get the door in the wall to open. He shook the doorknob. They screamed. Waking up early was a relief. Time to head back to Liberty Island.

AT SEA

E ven in late May, on the cusp of summer, it was chilly before
the sun rose. When Ryan arrived just past 5:00 A.M., the knot
of Highliners standing at the end of the wharf was breaking up,
each dispersing to their own boats. The diesel fumes of the *Sea
Angel*'s high exhaust pipe reached Ryan before he saw the boat,
tied up at the end of the wharf, its Cummins engine giving off a
low, contented bubbling hum.

Ryan stepped down into the *Sea Angel*. Caleb handed him a tall
one-quart thermos, saying, "This is yours for the day." The first
thing he noticed about the boat was that it was spick-and-span
clean. The white hull gleamed, with not a rust stain to be seen,
unusual for a working boat. And everything was in its place, tied
or snapped down, a physical illustration of shipshape. The second
thing he noticed was that all the newer lobster boats were open
at the stern—the better to work the sea, and then to hose out the
muck, pebbles, and assorted marine life that accumulated from
pulling lobster traps off the bottom.

Ryan poured out a cup from the thermos and sleepily sipped.
The taste shouted back: coffee, but not coffee.

Caleb looked at him, waiting. "First lesson," he explained as he pulled up the lines to the dock. The thermos contained the traditional lobsterman's breakfast, he said, "half a quart of hot milk, half a quart of coffee brandy." He added, "Usually taken along with some ibuprofen, if you're as old as me." Caleb couldn't be more than forty-five, Ryan thought. Caleb swung the wheel deftly so the bow moved out smartly. He gunned the engine and slipped by the stern of the boat in front of him with just inches to spare. It was clear he could do this with his eyes closed, just navigating by sound.

"Things to learn," Caleb announced, beginning the day's lessons as he turned into the Liberty Island Thorofare, heading west. "You need to know this island and its people. Begin with the history.

"Liberty Island has its own ways," he said. "These people here, they're not like your Puritans down in Boston. Different stock. Those Massachusetts people used to have names like Charity and Purity and Godfearing." He looked at Ryan. "Those people came from eastern England. They're farmers and brewers who settled the Massachusetts Bay Colony, the Plymouth Colony, and down the coast into Martha's Vineyard and Connecticut," he explained. "Religious hard-asses."

He turned to look at Ryan. "We're different. There's a reason we call people from down there 'Massholes.' Our people came from the fishing ports of the other side of England, the western and southern ports—Bristol, Plymouth. The guys here, the people you see in the Pal, we're descendants of hard men—soldiers who had survived the Revolutionary War and been given land grants, fishermen who worked their way over here through the gales of the North Atlantic, in wooden ships, with no GPS or radar or even decent maps. Their religion is different. Anyone who works the sea doesn't need a preacher's sermon to be told to fear God—they get reminded of it every day. Look at a forty-foot rogue wave coming at you when you're out to sea, you'll see the face of an angry God.

"When it was blowing too hard to fish, they worked the woods, hunting and felling trees. They made it through harsh winters by finding what was free and available: they chopped wood, they hauled buckets of salt water. If you had a good axe and a strong back, you could keep your cabin warm through the winter by boiling down that water continually and making salt, eventually getting enough to sell for a little cash money. In the old days, everyone knew the ratio, that four hundred gallons of seawater would boil down to sixty pounds of salt—that is, to one bushel. They got a few pennies for that.

"When times were hard, they could survive on the clams and mussels they dug from the muck. In the spring, they tapped maple trees and boiled the sap down to make sugar. More than one family survived those early springs, before the grass came up for the livestock, by living mainly on bread dipped in maple syrup. In the summer they picked raspberries, blueberries, blackberries. And when the weather cleared, they rowed out and took sturgeon and cod and lobsters."

"So not a lot of time for outsiders from other states?" Ryan said, half-jokingly.

"Hell," Caleb said, "we consider people from the rest of Maine to be outsiders. We say they are from 'off island.' Everyone else, from other states, they're 'people from away'—practically alien life forms." During colonial times and even after the Revolution, he said, the island had been called "Cumberland," after the claim on it by George II's third and favorite son. But in 1820, when Maine separated from Massachusetts to become its own state, islanders celebrated their newfound freedom by renaming it Liberty. "It stood for finally being their own people, not answering to the bloodsucking muckety-mucks down in Boston. To the island it meant freedom, independence, calling your own shots, and setting your own tax rates."

Caleb said a longtime summer neighbor of his, a lawyer from Philadelphia who had been a Peace Corps volunteer in India, had once told him that the island had its own caste system that reminded him of South Asia's. "We'd had a few beers, but as I remember it, he said we had five ranks, just like India. At the top were lobstermen, generally seen—especially by themselves—as the heart and soul of the place. He got that right.

"Below them, in the second rank, were other islanders, which by definition were people who had been born here, and probably their parents as well. In third place were Mainers who were not from the island. The fourth caste was people who lived here but were not native to the place—and would never be. Finally, in the fifth rank, there were short-term visitors, the day or week visitors. He said they were the equivalent of India's untouchables. I asked him what that meant, and he said, 'Their presence is tolerated only as long as they're spending money.' He was spot-on. We have a saying, 'If you're from Massachusetts, empty your wallet and go home.'

"My neighbor had thought about it a lot. He said that within each caste, there were hierarchies, which he said is also like India. Me, he said, 'You're a Highliner. That makes you a Brahmin, at the top rank of the top caste.' Below us comes the rank and file of fishermen, he figured. Bringing up the bottom, at the bottom rung of the first caste, are the less skilled fishermen. We call them 'dubs.'" Caleb looked over at Ryan. "That's not a nickname you want to get hung on you.

"This guy also said that in the fourth caste, the 'from-aways,' there are two ranks—'year-rounders,' people who had endured a few winters and stuck with it, and below them 'summer people,' who show up every year around July Fourth and disappear around Labor Day. He said the island puts up with them because they provide some entertainment and pay the property taxes that keep the streets plowed and the school system afloat—the island's two major public expenses. But he said those outsiders, no matter how wealthy, were locked in their low caste forever, and rarely would be invited into a higher-caste home." Caleb looked at Ryan. "When he said that, I realized that I was sitting in his yard drinking beer, and I like the guy, had known him for years, saw him every summer, and had never asked him into my house."

Ryan asked, "Did that make you feel bad?"

"Nah," Caleb said. "It's just the way things are. I think that's what he was saying."

Caleb turned the wheel to port and the boat leaned southward. Ryan extended a hand for support from the side of the wheelhouse as Caleb continued his historical introduction. "The men you see in the Pal are descendants of the early settlers," he said. "They earn their livings today like their ancestors did, with hooks, knives, ropes, hammers, and saws. They don't flinch at a little blood and pain on the job—the finger snagged on a fishhook, the thumb smashed in construction work, the chain saw that bucks into a shoulder while felling a tree. For fishermen, the occasional drowning. All in a day's work."

Caleb continued. "We have a code. No whining. Keep your word. If you say you're going to do something, do it. Work your job from dawn to dusk, and then do what the hell you like."

He looked over at Ryan. "It may sound rough, and odd, but it works," he added. "The island is pretty peaceful," he said. "Biggest problem is domestic violence."

"Wife beating?" Ryan asked. That word "rough" had struck Ryan as euphemistic, but he didn't say anything about that.

"The whole nine yards—spousal, child, elder. People know about it but are disinclined to intervene, 'cause you know 'a man's home is his castle,' as they say. They really believe that here. They'll say, 'She brought it on herself, needed a slap.' That's the way they were raised."

But there's other violence, Ryan thought. He asked: "What about the drug dealer from down around Boston who was killed here last year?" He had seen the incident summarized in his predecessor's file.

"That too." Caleb nodded. "Yep, that guy set up shop on Liberty early last year."

A few months later, the man's silver Cadillac ATS was found parked on Causeway Beach with its engine running. His body was lying across the back seat, hands and feet hog-tied together behind his back and a dryer hose running from the car's exhaust pipe into the window above him, duct-taped into place. It must have been an odd way to go, Ryan thought, the man lying there in the back seat, arms and legs tied behind him, growing sleepy from the monoxide, bright red blood dripping from his nose, feeling sleep wrapping its arms around him, and knowing death was imminent.

"Rough justice," Ryan said.

Caleb nodded again. "Island justice," he said, with a hint of approval. "It is different. Swift and sure. That's what you need to understand." He didn't tell Ryan that in his view, that incident itself wasn't a problem; it was something that ended a problem. No reason to provoke the FBI man.

"We're heading out to my fishing grounds," Caleb said. He explained that there was no law reserving one area for a given lobsterman. But, he said, in hard-nosed reality, everyone had their very specified fishing area, often passed down through several generations. Those who failed to recognize the unofficial but very real system soon found their trap lines tied with knots. If that warning sign wasn't heeded, their lines were cut, leaving their traps on the bottom. It was an expensive loss, with each outfitted trap and line costing as much as $200, and most men, and a few women, running at least four hundred traps.

Anyone foolish enough to persist after that ran into real damages. Last summer, for example, there had been a reckless new fisherman. He was from an island family, of course—anyone else wouldn't have been allowed to keep a lobster boat in the harbor. "No mooring spots available now," the harbormaster would say, "but I can put you on the waiting list"—which in fact did not exist. But this new young man had a hard time finding lobsters. Old hands, the semiretired skippers who spent their afternoons watching the world from benches on the docks of the co-ops, would mock him as he unloaded perhaps three dozen lobsters, a paltry take for a full day's work.

One day someone said mockingly, "Hey, kid, have you tried using bait?" The youth's face reddened. So to bolster his skimpy hauls, at odd moments when he thought no one was near, maybe when it was foggy, he began pulling some other guys' traps, taking just two or three lobsters from each.

One morning soon after that, he arrived at the commercial wharf only to look out and see that his boat had sunk at its mooring, its superstructure and antennas poking out above the waves. It had gone down in only about ten feet of water, but that was enough to ruin the electronics—radar, GPS display, depth finder, radios. That all amounted to a hefty bill. "The kid shaped up after some old hands talked to him," Caleb said. "He'll be okay." After making sure he understood the rules better, he said, they even scrounged up some used electronics for him so he could get back on his feet.

"If the rules are unwritten, how do you know them?" Ryan asked.

Caleb welcomed the question. This was why he had invited Ryan aboard the *Sea Angel*, his pride and joy, given that he was widowed and had no children. He was passionate about this. "For us," he said, "the rules, that's just common sense. It's the way the world works, or at least our part of it." You learned them by living here all your life, and your family too, for generations, maybe from stories your grandfather told you. "These rocks talk to me—that's where my uncle drowned, that's the sandbar where I took my wife for a picnic on our first date, there's the course my grandfather took across the Gulf of Maine during Prohibition to pick up Canadian whiskey in Nova Scotia." For those bootlegging trips, Caleb explained, Gramps would run over at night and sleep on the boat during the day while he waited for the liquor shipment. Then on the second night he would refuel the boat and run back to Liberty. He kept the bottles of booze submerged in extra traps, pulling them up as needed. "Lotta people on the island didn't believe that Prohibition applied here. And really, it didn't."

Caleb looked at Ryan. "And yes, it's a small world. When I walk into the Pal, I know everyone. Grew up with them. Dated their sisters. Played basketball with them. Gave them a hand one day when their engine froze up at sea. That waitress, Helen, who gave you grief? I pulled her Prius out of a ditch last winter when she had driven away drunk from home after her boyfriend smacked her. Faces I don't recognize in the Pal, those are from-aways—tourists or summer people."

Caleb paused. "Or, you know, maybe a federal agent," he said dryly. Then he went silent. Enough talk. And he needed to think about the day's work ahead of him.

Ryan admired the day as he sipped the mixture of coffee brandy and milk, bringing a warm glow to his stomach. Seals sunning on rocks watched the boat pass. Caleb pointed to a huge osprey nest atop a tall spruce on an islet. One of the parents, likely the mother, gazed back at them. A flock of small guillemots, black-and-white waterfowl the size of doves but rounder, noisily flapped and swam out of the path of the boat.

The boat's hull skipped and thumped over the low waves. "Feel that grinding in your knee joints?" Caleb said. "Fiberglass hulls last forever, but at a price: They transmit every bump and thump right up your legs into your knees, just chews away at the bones." By contrast, he said, wooden boats, used only by "real old-timers," were slower and more expensive to maintain, but absorbed more of the shocks of the sea, instead of passing them up into your bones. Aside from messing with your joints, Caleb added, the *Sea Angel* was "a right comfortable vessel, steady, dependable, and safe."

When they were about fifteen miles south of Liberty, Caleb jabbed a gloved finger down at the paper chart thumbtacked to the bulkhead. "Where my ancestors settled." His boat had all the current GPS maps, radar display, and depth finders, but he liked to keep the old paper chart in sight for context. You could make quick marks with it using the pencil stub hanging on a dirty string.

Ryan peered down at it. "Goodwin Island?" he read aloud. "That's your family?"

Caleb nodded. Ryan considered the map for a moment. That island was remote. "Why so far out?"

Before the internal combustion engine, Caleb explained, you either sailed a small sloop or rowed a dory to your fishing grounds. So there was an advantage in living on an island out to sea—you could get to the grounds faster, spend more time productively fishing, and get home to safety quickly if the weather turned. "They lived here for 136 years," he said. "Might go up to Liberty Harbor once a week for mail and supplies."

"What happened?" Ryan asked.

"The Depression and Boston bankers," he said. "Back then, no one had any cash around here. You could survive on foraging and bartering, but people didn't have the cash to pay tax bills." His family had lost the island for nonpayment of property taxes, while the bankers sniffed through the town records and snapped up delinquent properties. "Some hedge fund manager owns it now. Met him once. Kind of thin, awkward, and goofy. Not good for anything but investment banking, I guess." On the island, a man who did not work with his hands was viewed with suspicion, like he wasn't really pulling his weight. More to be pitied than envied, no matter how much money he pocketed from his job. Can't buy respect, at least not on Liberty, the saying went. You earned it by putting your back into your work, not by juggling little colored numbers displayed on laptops. What kind of work was that?

They arrived where all the lobster buoys bobbing in the sea were painted black-and-green, the same as the buoy displayed above the cabin of the *Sea Angel*. This was Goodwin's area. They talked as he began to pull and inspect traps.

"Tell me about Ricky Cutts," Ryan said.

Caleb instead winched up a trap made of galvanized steel wire coated in yellow vinyl, threw out three smaller lobsters, and put rubber bands on the claws of two keepers. Ryan was momentarily surprised to see that they were mottled black and dark green, not red, as he kind of had expected. He kept that to himself. Caleb inserted a new bait bag into the trap and shoved it over the side, back into the sea.

After pulling six more traps with similarly low results, Caleb was ready to talk again. "Ricky? He's an island boy. Well, not a boy. But never quite grew up, you know. Always got mad too fast. His old man made him work for him on his boat, didn't pay him. Knocked him around a bit. When I was a kid, half the time when I saw Ricky, he'd have a black eye and a kind of beaten-dog look to him."

After Ricky's father died, Ricky took over the boat. Did okay, eventually got himself a new one. "*Pussy Man*?" asked Ryan.

"Yes, unfortunate name," Caleb said, giving a headshake of disapproval. "But typical of Ricky. Always in your face." He pulled another trap. This one had a huge lobster in it, perhaps five pounds. Caleb held it up to show Ryan, the huge greenish-black claws, each the size of a man's hand, waving in anguish or anger. Volcano-like white barnacles stood on the backs of the claws. "This one's an old man," he said, "maybe thirty years old or more." He pointed to one claw, longer and thinner than the other: "That's the slasher. He can cut you bad."

"And the other?" asked Ryan, looking at the fatter, thicker claw.

"Even worse," said Caleb. "That's the crusher. You don't want to get a finger in there."

"That must be a real keeper," Ryan said, admiringly.

"Nope. Not legal, and for good reason," Caleb said. The bigger, older lobsters, anything bigger than about three pounds, were off-limits in order to preserve the breed stock. Also, he said, any egger—a lobster bearing hundreds of tiny, caviar-like eggs—was returned to the sea. "The fellows down in southern New England didn't do that. We did. They killed off their fishery, while our approach has kept the Maine lobster industry thriving for a century," he said. He dropped the monster gently back into the sea. "A few guys up here might keep 'em, call 'em 'boot lobsters,' because they carry them off the boat in their fishing boots, so no one sees them. But most of us know better."

"Some guys like Ricky Cutts?" Ryan asked, pushing the conversation back to the issue of the day.

Caleb stared into the distance. He thought for a moment. "Yeah," he said evenly, "guys who are like Ricky. There's always one or two of them around, it seems."

He knew why Ryan was on his boat. And he was ready to talk about Ricky now. He sighed and shook his head. "Ricky was always looking for shortcuts, to get a leg up, like he had decided he couldn't make it in this world following the rules. I think that was the lesson his father beat into him, that he was never gonna be good enough to make it unless he cut corners. There are just some guys like that."

"That enough to get him killed?" Ryan asked.

"No, it isn't" Caleb said. "But with a guy like Ricky, you never know who he's pissed off. Sometimes it's drugs. Sometimes it's fishing arguments. Or an angry father or brother. What I think is, someone got sick of his shit." He pulled back on the throttle of the engine, and the diesel roar ended the conversation. The bow rose up as the engine's five hundred horses pushed the boat to its full twenty knots. At the northern end of his grounds, the very edge of where he fished, he slowed and dumped a string of six traps. "Just camping them here," he said, using the term for a lobsterman marking his territory even if he didn't expect the traps to be immediately productive. "There are some crevices down there that will be crawling with lobsters come summer, and I plan to get them." He felt the need to preemptively reassert his claim to that area because it was on the very periphery of his family's traditional ground. Timid fishermen did not thrive.

After setting that string and marking its location on his GPS, Caleb steered northeast—that is, away from his home harbor. He slowed the boat and asked Ryan to go below for the hunting rifle. "Hanging in the bag above the port side bunk."

Down in the trunk cabin, Ryan looked around and saw that everything was tidy. There were two bunks, each with warm wool blankets folded and zippered into clear plastic bags that keep out the salty sea air. Between them was a diesel-fueled space heater. On the walls were pegs for the fishermen's slickers. Under the bunks were plastic boxes filled with gloves and boots, a box of plastic bottles of engine oil, and about fifty coils of spare rope. A large blue toolbox, a full yard long, was held in place by wooden brackets—the last thing a skipper wanted in a blow was seventy pounds of expensive tools crashing around below. Everything was in its place, and there was a place for everything. Ryan took the green nylon rifle bag off its hooks above the bunk, unzipped it, and lifted out the weapon, which was rolled in lightly oiled cloth to further protect it from the salt air, which would be ruinous to the delicate steel mechanisms of the rifle. It was a bolt action .270 Winchester.

When he came back up on deck, Caleb was bringing the *Angel* alongside a dock on a small island. They had experienced a lousy day of fishing, pulling a hundred traps and keeping the ninety lobsters that met the regulations. "This early in the season, it barely pays the cost of going out," Caleb said. "But you fish your ground partly to maintain a clear claim. And there are other compensations." With his left hand, he took a box of cartridges from a plastic bag in his lunch box while turning the boat's wheel with his right. He tied up the boat at the dock, hopped up onto it, grabbed a loop of rope that was hanging on the dock's railing, and began walking up to the land. "Bring the rifle, would you?" he said over his shoulder.

"This is Goodwin Island," Caleb said. "That's his house," he said, pointing at a sprawling multimillion-dollar version of an old shingled Maine cottage. But, he added, the investment banker never came up from New York until mid-July. "Won't be here for another six weeks or so."

Past the house, they followed a mossy path into the spruce woods. Caleb took the Winchester, loaded it, and put his finger to his lips. "I see deer out on this point all the time," he said softly. "If we don't thin the herds, they starve in winter." He instructed Ryan to walk fifty feet to his left. "Don't get ahead of me, stay on my flank, and always within my sight." Together they would herd the deer toward the open meadow at the southern end of the small island.

At first the only sound was the light whistling of the low wind through the needles of the spruce and fir. Then Ryan heard a hurried crunching in the woods, and saw a flash of a white tail. Then a crash through bushes and branches. To his right, Caleb fired once, dropping a doe with a solid shot just behind and below the shoulder—that is, straight through the heart. Caleb hurried up to the dead deer and knelt by it. The fishing knife flashed out of its sheath on his hip and slit the animal's throat. Caleb tied a quick bowline knot around the deer's rear hooves, then dragged the dead animal to the shade under a solitary maple tree. He flung the rope over a low limb, hoisted the deer, tied off the rope on a maple trunk, and let the animal's blood drain out.

"Good shot," Ryan said, genuinely impressed. He heard a flapping and looked up to see crows gathering on the tree's upper limbs. They were cawing loudly, spreading the news of an imminent feast. Crows, who are the most intelligent of birds, had watched and learned the routine: a shot heard on an outer island usually meant a good meal was about to appear. Within fifteen minutes Caleb had the animal butchered, with the tenderloin, filets, and steaks wrapped in plastic shopping bags. He left the rest for the two dozen crows who were walking and talking impatiently above them, sorting out their pecking order.

As the two men walked back to the boat, the crows descended behind them onto the glistening ribs and shanks, with some fighting over the intestines. "Most of this meat I'll take to families that need it," Caleb said. "You got to watch out for people, especially the old folks. Fresh venison is good for them, full of nutrients, especially a rich load of vitamin C. That's a big reason the Indians didn't get scurvy, that and the pemmican they chewed in winter." He said he also would drop a few cuts with Louise at Sarah's Shelter.

But not all of it would go to the needy. At the dock, Caleb handed him a filet to take home to Bangor for his dinner. "Might help strengthen your knees," Caleb said. He explained: "You're gonna need it after a full day on the boat. No more than four minutes a side, okay? Some sauteed onions will cover most of the evergreen taste."

Sitting in the cab of his truck, Ryan made his calls. First was to Johnny Mac, the tribal policeman on Malpense Island. Off to Augusta tomorrow, Mac replied, but on Malpense the day after. "About Ricky Cutts and his boat," Ryan offered.

Even over the phone, Ryan could sense Johnny Mac's reserve and distance. The aloofness echoed through in his voice. He had the average Mainer's suspicion of outsiders, combined with the average First Peoples' wariness of Anglos, as they called all people of different ethnicity from them. And he had a caginess all his own.

"Yeah, I know him," Mac finally offered about Cutts. "He comes by out here sometimes."

Then Ryan called the cell of the Park Service liaison officer. Yes, she said, they could have a boat take him down to Malpense, from the Bass Harbor wharf. Ryan took down the details.

His third call was to the FBI office in Baltimore, asking if they could find anything about the estranged wife of one Ricky Cutts.

The only music Ryan played in his truck was the greatest hits of Hank Williams. On the drive back to Bangor, Hank sang, "Take my advice or you'll curse the day you started rollin' down that lost highway."

Once home, he realized he hadn't checked his mailbox by the paved road in weeks. He opened it and found several letters from the lawyer in San Diego, as well as a package from Wundermin, his old supervisor in that city. It contained a book—*Man's Search for Meaning*, by Viktor Frankl. How long had it been waiting there? Ryan found a note slipped inside: "Ryan—This was valuable to me at a difficult time in my life. I hope it might help you. You are now a survivor, and that is a big load to carry. SAC Wundermin." It struck him that the special agent in charge signed the note as if "SAC" were his first name.

Going up the cottage's front stairs, Ryan felt the promised light ache in his knees. He opened a bottle of Bogle merlot and grilled the venison on the stove. He didn't have any onions on hand. Light aroma, almost veal like, but with a definite tang of spruce to it. Real woods food. He put it between two pieces of toast with mayonnaise and ate it as a sandwich on the deck overlooking the pond. Only then, slowly chewing and relishing each rich bite, did it occur to him that legal deer season wasn't for another six months. He seemed to be adjusting to the ways of Liberty Island. He paged through his notes for the day.

That night, his dream was like a documentary film. He was sitting at his desk in the FBI's San Diego field office, doing expense accounts, the bane of his life. He was always behind on those. He looked up and saw the special agent in charge of the field office standing over him. "Come with me," SAC Wundermin ordered.

Ryan stood and followed him to the elevator. Wordlessly they descended to the shadows of the parking garage. They walked through the half light to Wundermin's huge black Chevrolet Tahoe. The entire office staff could fit into that thing. "Get in," he said. Once they were seated in it, Wundermin turned and said he had bad news, that Ryan's wife, Marta, and both children had been in a car crash. "Looks bad," he added.

It was worse than that—much worse. His wife, on her way home from work, had just picked up the kids at their church's day care center. Driving across the four-lane road, her SUV was T-boned by a construction trucker hauling dirt who didn't see the red stoplight. He hadn't even braked. The heavily laden truck plowed the SUV down the road, flipped it, then rolled over on top of it. Two Jaws of Life teams were needed to remove the bodies. At the hospital, Ryan and Wundermin were directed to the emergency room, and from there to the adjacent morgue. There, laid out on three steel tables under green sheets, were the bodies of his wife and the children. On a fourth table, oddly, lay the family's yellow Labrador, without a sheet, blood dripping from its jaws. Without knowing why, he focused on the dog's presence. He realized it was being preserved as part of an investigation. In the morning his wife and children had been his family. Now they had been transformed into cold "evidence."

Ryan's knees buckled, and he fell into a vortex of grief. It was then he began to ride the Tilt-A-Whirl of death, as he came to think of it in the following weeks—that nauseating spin of anger, grief, and disorientation. It was worse when he lay down, so he had learned to sleep sitting in his living room's armchair. But it wasn't really sleep as much as exhaustion and semiconsciousness.

He awoke in a sweat and showered, eager to get away from that dream. One thing he liked about Maine was that he hadn't seen a single parking garage since starting work there.

MAJOR CRIMES UNIT

I n the morning Ryan decided to look into the details of the death
by monoxide on Liberty Island of Mitch Dondi, the drug dealer
from near Boston. He called Luther Parmenter, his contact at the
Hancock County sheriff's office, who said that investigation was
being handled by the State Patrol's Major Crimes Unit in Bangor.
Two more calls led him to the northern unit's sole homicide investigator, a Lieutenant D'Agostino.

"FBI? Bangor? No shit? Didn't know they had someone up
here," the homicide detective said when Ryan identified himself.

An hour later, Ryan sat down across from the lieutenant at a
gray metal desk in the State Police barracks. The Dondi investigation was an open case, D'Agostino began. "Gotta warn you, you're
looking into that, you're not gonna get far on Liberty Island,"
he said, in a world-weary way. "Usually, we bust someone for
coke possession, meth, they'll roll over on who sold it to them.
Not those island people—they'll fight it all the way. No one
talks, they contest the charges, then they'll request a jury trial,
and finally, if on the off chance we get the jury to convict, they
just ride out the jail time. So yeah, our conviction rates on island
cases kind of suck."

D'Agostino filled him in on the basics of the Dondi case, then gave a world-class shrug, shoulders lifting and arms outstretched, apparently in frustration. "Bottom line," he said, "down there, our basic tools of investigation don't work. We know this Mitch Dondi sold dope on the island, but I never managed to get much on the other end of the transactions—you know, the buyers—to play ball." The state patrolman's hands, now back on the desk, tightened into fists. "It always got me that the perps didn't burn Dondi's stubby little Cadillac. That tells me they wanted this action to be seen—noticed, you know? And they didn't see a need to cover their tracks."

Sounds like they were right, Ryan thought. But no reason to antagonize D'Agostino with that particular observation.

D'Agostino said that it was getting near time to move the Dondi inquiry to cold cases—formally, the "unsolved homicides." There was always hope that someone caught for something else would tell the police. "Cellmate informants, you know. But you know, no one wants to spend a lot of the taxpayers' money on figuring out who killed a drug dealer. Maybe another drug dealer. Maybe a pissed off parent. What's the difference?"

Ryan asked if he could look at the Dondi file. "Hell, you can take it with you. Knock yourself out. Return it when you can. No hurry." He pushed a brown accordion folder across the desktop, as if encouraging it to leave. It was just a nagging reminder of failure. Ryan looked inside. There were a few photos of the crime scene and a thin manila file. Ryan flipped through the list of interviewees on the first page. No names jumped out at him. It was a different world. It looked to be a roster of small-time users.

"Cell phone?" asked Ryan.

"Didn't find one," the detective said. "We know he owned several, under different names, changed them out every couple of days. We got some numbers, tracked them down. Just found some of the usual dopeheads, plus a younger crowd that was new to us."

Ryan stood with the folder under his arm. Last thing: "Ever come across a guy named Ricky Cutts?"

"Nope."

"Abby Buck?"

Another headshake. D'Agostino said, "Can I ask you a question?"

"Sure," Ryan said. He suspected what was coming.

D'Agostino leaned forward and said, "Is there a story behind your being assigned here?"

"Some other time," Ryan said. "Thanks."

At home he sat down on the back porch to study the folder. The chronology page showed twenty hours of desultory police inquiries over the course of four days. The most interesting aspect was a printout of Mitch's criminal record. He had been busted at the age of eighteen for narcotics distribution in Revere, Massachusetts. A year later, his older brother was found dead, floating face down just west of that town in Rumney Marsh near the Salem Turnpike Bridge. A birdwatcher had noticed an osprey pecking on the back of his neck. After that incident, Mitch moved up I-95 to Gloucester, Massachusetts, and then to Portsmouth, New Hampshire. He was busted there and later in Portland, Maine; Brunswick, Maine; Friendship, Maine; and Belfast, Maine. Several arrests were followed by spells of increasing length in the detention facilities of each state. After his last release he had moved on to Liberty Island. He basically had failed his way up the New England coast, as he supplied drugs to the fishermen, the dock workers, the tugboat crews, and others in the maritime trades.

Ryan was unimpressed by the file. There was no log of who else had been present at the crime scene, just the name of Lt. D'Agostino. Nor were there reports from a crime lab or an inventory of property found in the car. The medical examiner's report, signed by a Dr. Aziz, at least confirmed that the cause of death was forcible asphyxiation by monoxide—that is, the car exhaust piped into the car in which he was tied up in the back seat. *Pretty thin stuff,* Ryan thought.

OUT TO MALPENSE

That afternoon at Bass Harbor, the Park Service boat was waiting, the big brown shield painted on its side. Standing on the wharf next to it was the same ranger Ryan had dealt with on Isle au Haut. He was casually smoking a joint.

There were three big, distant offshore islands along this stretch of Maine coast: Monhegan, Matinicus, and Malpense. Monhegan had become a tourist island, the visitors lured there by the artists who loved to study the late-afternoon light sloping across the ocean to the island, one of the few places on the East Coast of the United States where the sunset light could come in unimpeded for well over one hundred miles. The second, Matinicus, had remained solidly in the hands of the local fishing community, and not even yachts were made particularly welcome, let alone ferryboat day-trippers.

The third island, farther to the east and a bit to the south, was Malpense, the most remote and wildest of them all. It had an air of legend to it, because so few people, and even fewer non-Mainers, had ever landed on it. The island had no ferry service, nor any stores at its little harbor. Indeed, NOAA chart 13312, which covered the area around Malpense, contained among its abundant small type a terse notice, printed in light purple, to mariners that "vessels should avoid entering tribal waters protected under treaty clauses. Illegal to fish or land at harbor without written permission in advance from tribal authorities."

Malpense had remained outside the grasp of the big world. It was a tribal possession, and no wonder. Well over the horizon from the mainland, it had a fortress-like feel to it—sheer granite cliffs on the south and east, and shoal ground to the west that, in a high wind, could rip the bottom off a boat in a few minutes. Yet on its north side, it unexpectedly offered a pocket harbor, curving in like a *J*. In most weather, this little inlet was entirely protected from the prevailing winds and also from the storms that might swirl in from the south or east. And the peculiar shape of the tiny harbor even offered some protection from the worst of the winter's fierce northwest winds, screaming out of the Canadian Arctic amid razor-sharp cold fronts.

Despite the little harbor, Malpense Island remained barely inhabited. Three tribal clans—Wolf, Shark, and Owl—had family branches out there, most of them staying only for the three fishing seasons, with just a caretaker remnant left of two or three to see the place through the winter.

As the Park Service boat approached Malpense, Ryan thought it looked entirely forbidding, not yet seeing that its northern shore held a snug harbor. Additionally grim was a large red-and-white sign that he saw posted on a buoy: WARNING! TRIBAL WATERS. DO NOT PROCEED WITHOUT PERMISSION.

Underneath this was painted, in red, a long two-pronged fishing spear. That was the symbol of the southern branch of the Malpense, while the northern branch's signs featured both a spear and a hunting arrow. "Southern branch is small but frisky, acts kind of independent," the ranger commented as they passed the cautionary sign.

The narrow, crevice-like harbor was barely wide enough for a boat to turn. At its end, standing atop the harbor's sole dock, was Johnny Mac. He probably had heard the engine coming in. Island people can recognize individual boats by the sound they make. Behind him stood a handful of buildings—shacks, really, for summer living and eating. Fishing nets hung on their outside walls, the better to let the rain wash out the corrosive salt, and also to hold them in place for inspection and the inevitable small repairs on their mesh.

It was near low tide, so the subchief up on the dock loomed ten feet above the boat. He pointed behind a twenty-five-foot Boston Whaler marked TRIBAL POLICE. "Tie up there," he instructed. They climbed up the dock ladder to meet him.

Ryan couldn't detect any expression on the subchief's face. Two younger men sat on blue plastic bait barrels a few feet away, idly watching the two Anglos. Johnny Mac didn't so much welcome Ryan and the ranger as accept their presence.

"Agent Tapia, you are now standing on the territory of the Malpense Nation," he said impassively. "We consent to your presence as a courtesy between law enforcement officers. You are pursuing a federal homicide investigation, but other than that, lacking a warrant duly issued by the elders of the tribal court, you carry no powers or jurisdiction here. I will show you my tribe's traditional courtesy toward good faith visitors, and so will help you to the extent I can."

"Got it," Ryan said. "Not looking for trouble, just here to examine Ricky Cutts's boat." The subchief pointed over to it. FV *Pussy Man* was hauled up on the inner bar, winched up there at high tide. Ryan was no expert in lobster boats, but in his time in the navy he had learned enough to know that Cutts's boat was a sad sight. Its red hull needed paint, with the white fiberglass showing through in many places. Orange streaks of rust stained the hull below each cleat and each vertical of the bow railing. The radio antenna was held in place only with the aid of a generous wrapping of silver duct tape around a crutch stick and a rope tethering it to a forward cleat, making a hazard for anyone moving around the bow area. White barnacles and black mussel shells dotted the bottom half of the stern, sending up a stench as they died from being out of the sea. And there was long green kelp on the hull, now drying and shriveling to brown, giving off its own sulfurous smell.

"Let's do it," the chief said, inviting himself to join the search. "I'll get some tools."

Ryan thought of telling him to back off, but stopped himself. After all, he reasoned to himself, the boat had been here for days. The chief could have done with it what he wanted. And there was no reason to be impolite.

Behind the boat stood Mac's work shed, its double doors swung open for the day's work. The tools hung neatly in rows on the three walls. On the outside of the shed, facing the afternoon sun, were three planks with big fish pegged to them. The third fish, the biggest, perhaps six feet long, looked like some kind of prehistoric beast, with a scaled olive-green back, a white belly, and an ugly shovel-like snout. The ranger followed Ryan's eye. "That's two good-looking cod and, him, the dinosaur-looking fellow, that's an Atlantic sturgeon," the ranger said. "The Malpense say their treaty allows them to fish out of season, and even to take fish that are protected from fishing, as long as they fish for sustenance." He pointed to the dinosaur-looking fish. "The sturgeon was also known as 'the King's fish,'" he said, because in England, a medieval law had required that all sturgeon caught had to be delivered immediately into royal hands. "The colonists, they come over here, they can't believe that anyone was allowed to eat them.

"Marine biologists will tell you that this fish is extinct in Maine's coastal waters," the ranger added. "But as you can see, they're wrong. Maybe they don't know where to look, or no one will tell them."

The subchief appeared with a hammer, a set of socket wrenches, and two marine crowbars—short versions, the better for working inside the tight spaces of a boat. He had heard the ranger's comment. "That's right," he said. "Legal, as long as we consume them ourselves. And they're damn good eating, sweet white boneless flesh. If we're lucky, caviar too."

They climbed up onto the stern of the abused vessel. The FV *Pussy Man* was a mess, even before it became a drifter. They started with the engine. The oil in the crankcase was sludgy and filthy and the fuel filters just as bad. "You gotta wonder where this guy bought his diesel, how long it had been sitting," Johnny Mac said. "Probably has algae in the fuel lines." The boat was worse for the recent wear. Someone had stripped out the two VHF radios, radar, GPS system, and monitor for the bottom scanner. The forward cabin, just past the helm, needed a good cleaning. Its main features were empty cans of beer and potato chip bags. *Not even any pornography*, Ryan thought, then realized that might have been snatched up along with the electronics.

"His fishing grounds aren't far from here," Johnny, the subchief, said, explaining that Cutts had been an occasional visitor. "He was off to the west, other side of Big Bold Island." He waved his left arm out in the direction of that island. "Might pull in here to get out of the way of a squall, or if he had engine trouble. He might have fish we'd want, trade him for fuel." He paused, then added, "But we never invited him to overnight here."

Ryan asked why Ricky wasn't ever invited to stay.

"Well," the subchief said, "with Ricky there also was a basic problem. In one of our stories about the Mischief Maker, there's a phrase, 'angry with the sun and at war with all people.' Ricky was like that. He was trouble. A skirmisher. A low-grade scammer, always looking for an angle. Type of guy, supposed to deliver someone an ounce of coke, he'd take a snort for himself. I told him to keep his drugs off my island."

"Did he?"

"Usually. But that meant he could just sell the stuff from the boat, meet up out there," the subchief said, nodding in the direction of the open sea.

In the forward cabin, Ryan opened a dented old brown metal tool kit. There was the usual jumble of screws, screwdrivers, spark plugs, ratchet wrench fittings—all out of order here, metric and American jumbled together—plus the basic seagoing necessities, such as hooks and line. And in the right-hand top compartment lay a row of small plastic packets containing white powder.

"See, that's the problem," Johnny added, with a thus-it-is-proven tone in his voice.

They each took a short crowbar, the kind called a pry bar, and began peeling back the plastic sideboards. Ryan started with one board that looked well worked, like it had been opened more than a sideboard usually would require. Sitting inside the compartment was a double-bagged pile of yellow rock meth, perhaps an ounce. Ryan's initial impulse was to bag and tag the drugs as potential evidence. But of course, he remembered, he lacked jurisdiction. He was only here for a murder investigation.

Ryan took a moment to reassess the subchief: (1) Motive?—doesn't want drugs on the island; (2) Means?—knows how and where to waylay Cutts on the water. Take his boat, strip it, say it washed up here; (3) Opportunity?—ample.

Ryan didn't realize he was staring. Johnny coolly returned the gaze, his face blank except for a cocked eyebrow. "No, Mister FBI,

I didn't do it. Got better things to do. But I can see why someone might." He stopped. He had said what he needed to say.

Ryan thanked the subchief for his time and climbed into the Park Service boat for the run back north to Bass Harbor. The man didn't say goodbye; he just stood at the end of the dock with his arms crossed, and nodded to acknowledge their departure. He had something on his mind.

WHAT PEELED PAUL SAW

Johnny was thinking about what he hadn't told them, which was what he had heard from Peeled Paul. *But*, he thought, *they hadn't asked.*

Paul Soco was a tribal member whose life had fragmented in his late twenties. That was a surprise, because he had started well. He played basketball in high school, that tough sport that helps a lot of people get through the winter in Maine. He was not tall, but the Maine version of the sport had rugby-like characteristics that rewarded a player willing to take a hit and able to deliver some as well. Unfortunately, after those hard-fought games, some of his teammates taught him how to drink alcohol. From there he went to Washington County Community College in Calais. After graduating he became a shop and industrial arts teacher at a high school and coached junior varsity basketball. He also taught a course on the maintenance of motorcycles and snowmobiles that was so popular it had a waiting list.

Most of all, he loved working with wood, being alone with the grain, helping reveal the beauty of it. He told himself that teaching would be great if he just didn't have to deal with students. He had never been quite at ease in the world, either the tribal one or the other larger one outside the reservation. He was drinking a lot of alcohol every night, which angered his teetotaling father. "Whiskey ruined many of our people, took many of my friends, and I fear you are becoming one more walking ghost," his father said sadly one morning as Paul moped with a hangover at the breakfast table. He reminded Paul that it was not allowed in their house. His father also was becoming increasingly erratic with old age, with great squalls of anger that came and went within a few minutes.

Paul was sweet on a young woman, Darla, who worked at the tribe's day care center. He met her one day while dropping off one of his younger students who was picking up a sibling. She seemed quiet and nice, so he went by a couple more times to chat, but hadn't worked up the courage to ask her on a date. Her name, it turned out, had been given to her by her mother after a favorite character in the *Our Gang* short comedy films. The reruns of those shows were carried every day at four in the afternoon on a secondary Bangor television station under the name *The Little Rascals with Lumberjack Bob*, who actually was the station's weatherman, doing the double duty that came with broadcasting in the boonies.

Finally, one wet and windy Monday afternoon, Paul went by the center to ask Darla out. He already had made a reservation for that Friday at the Riverview Restaurant in Calais, the favored date restaurant in the area. The woman at the front desk didn't look up at him. "Darla?" she said. "Died over the weekend. OD." She added that the funeral was on Friday. Paul didn't know that by the day of that service, he would be behind bars in the tribal jail.

Paul, deeply shaken, drove to the mobile home he shared with his father to find the old man standing on the front steps. He was yelling and waving a bottle of Johnnie Walker Red at him. Paul had stashed it under his bed and forgotten about it. His father swung the bottle by the neck at Paul, who tried to restrain him.

The two tumbled down the stairs. His father took the worst of it, as Paul's weight landed on him. The father wound up hospitalized with neck and back injuries. Renny Sanpeer, the tribal police chief, took Paul into custody.

When his father died ten days later, the Tribal Council decided to try Paul. His offense had occurred entirely among tribal members on tribal lands, so the state lacked jurisdiction. The Council's verdict was that the act had been inadvertent but that penance was due and time for healing was needed. They sentenced Paul to a year's reflective isolation. He was to serve it on Big Bold, the southwesternmost island the tribe possessed, about two miles west of Malpense. It was a good-sized but virtually inaccessible island, with no harbor, nor even an inlet or cove, surrounded on every side by sloping rock. But at its center, at the top of a small hill, it did have a small tide-driven spring—that is, as the tide came in, the huge weight of the incoming seawater pressed on the fresh water table below the sea and forced some up. Twice a day, a person could collect as much water as needed, albeit a bit brackish at the beginning of the flow. Let it sit for twenty-four hours in a jug, and it was perfectly drinkable.

Johnny Mac took him out there, towing a rowboat that contained all that would be needed to physically sustain Paul—a sleeping bag, a hundred-pound bag of rice, five gallons of cooking oil, cooking pots, a hunting knife, a Winchester rifle, ammunition, five lobster traps, hooks and line, an axe, a shovel, a tree-cutting saw, and five hundred feet of nylon rope. That first night a heavy rainstorm rolled in. Paul spent the night sleeping under the rowboat. In the morning he began building a small lean-to and a deep firepit.

Settling into a hermit's existence on the island, Paul discovered depths of reserves in himself that he had not known were there. Once a week a boat from Malpense Island would stop off with a bag of fruit and vegetables and whatever tools he had requested. He paid for those with some of the harvest of his hunting. At first, Paul would hear their boat coming and row out to meet them in the small boat that he laboriously hauled down the rock to the water. Soon he built a little double-tracked wooden skid for it from cedar and rope, enabling him to hop into the rowboat at the top of the rock and slide thirty feet down in it to the water. Then he constructed a winch system to pull it back up the rails. By midsummer he stopped wearing clothes, hence the "Peeled" nickname the other Malpense gave to him, which other fishermen soon adopted. It stuck because it not only was about his lack of clothes, but the way he seemed to have shed some of the debilitating ways of modern civilization.

He shot deer on adjacent islands and smoked most of the meat to preserve it for later consumption. He pulled his lobster traps, ate the lobsters, and kept the side catch for bait. He spearfished wolffish and cod. He hook fished for halibut, and mackerel. He built a fish weir between two islets and was pleasantly surprised to find it brought him an occasional haddock. At the intermittent spring he dug a holding pool to capture the water when it was forced up and to let it settle and clear. He cornered and killed over two hundred ducks during their short flightless phase in late summer when their new feathers come in. He made brined jerky of their meat. Using a canvas sail he'd found washed up, so old that after a long soak in spring water it became soft and pliable, he sewed together a large and enormously warm comforter that he filled with the ducks' downy feathers.

One clear August night, when the moon was full, he was awakened to an eerie but pleasant sound similar to electronic music, a high humming and whistling with an occasional click. He walked down to the water below his lean-to. There, just offshore, he saw a pod of whales resting on the surface and singing together in the brilliant moonlight. They were all pointed toward the sheen of the moon. He felt he was being allowed by some rare act of grace to observe the religious services of another species.

His days were full, even urgent. He was either eating, working to get more food, or building something. He moved from one task to another from sunup to sundown. While fishing and hunting, he kept an eye out for rocks that could go into a foundation or chimney. "It was a time to gather stones together"—this was a phrase he remembered from an old pop song. When he had a high pile of those accumulated, he enclosed the lean-to. Then he built a bigger room next to it with a stone foundation and a stone chimney, and turned the existing room into his storage space. He cut and roughly milled some maple trees for the floor of the new cabin. When he felt energetic, he built. When he was fatigued, he sat in the rowboat and fished. At night he sat before the fire and thought through the next day's tasks. When he lay down and closed his eyes, he fell asleep instantly. He dreamed of Darla. Like her, he had gone to another world.

When winter came Paul surprised everyone again by toughing it out. He began wearing clothes again, but he never asked the Tribal Council that he be allowed to leave Big Bold before serving out his full sentence. He accepted the gifts the Council sent his way—a secondhand down parka, work gloves, new long underwear, and insulated boots. He declined the old chain saw that was sent as "too noisy." He had come to revel in the silence of the island, especially at night, when it was just him between the waves breaking below and a powerful array of stars floating above. The Milky Way became like a familiar friend.

His life felt better, more real, saner, than ever before. During the long, warm summer evenings he had sometimes worked until ten at night. During the deepest part of winter, by contrast, he almost hibernated, sleeping twelve hours at a spell. Then he would awaken and circumambulate the island, checking the snow for animal tracks, often while being followed by a friendly woodpecker who flew from branch to branch.

At the end of his year's sentence, he simply stayed on the island. The Tribal Council noted this but was not perturbed. This was, for once, a ruling that had served its intended purpose. Paul had found satisfaction, even peace.

The southern subtribe, not unhappy with his decision to stay, designated him official caretaker of Big Bold. Having him stand watch on the periphery of their possessions was helpful, especially if outside fishing boats began nosing around the deep channel where the sturgeon dwelled. The Malpense boats delivered saws and shovels, nails, screws, and cement. The tribe also gave him a set of binoculars and budgeted $250 a month as his pay, which covered the cost of the food, tools, and other supplies they brought him. He in turn gave them gifts of duck jerky and otter pelts. They wanted him to have a two-way radio, but he declined so instead they gave him a red tribal flag to hoist if he saw danger. To celebrate his new position, he built a ladder on one of the tallest pines, the better to climb up and post that flag if ever needed. He felt like he was ruler of his one-man land.

The other day, when Johnny Mac had run over with the usual load of supplies, they had chatted about the fishing and about what he had been seeing. Paul said he had been pulling in a cod when he had seen a lobster boat motor down and tie up to Ricky Cutts's, maybe a mile to the west of Big Bold, just outside tribal waters. Stayed just for a minute, which was normal if a guy was just dropping off something, like a needed motor part or tool. But what was odd was that after the white boat left, Ricky Cutts's boat just drifted north and east. It was hard to tell at that distance, but Paul didn't think anyone was at the helm of Cutts's boat. "I wanted to tell you about it because it seemed kind of funny to me," Paul said. Johnny Mac didn't want Paul to get involved. He replied noncommittally that you never knew what lobstermen were up to. But he filed away the information in the back of his mind.

Paul said he was considering taking up bow hunting, because it was so much quieter than shooting. "Good for you," Johnny Mac said. "I admire your approach to life."

The FBI man hadn't asked if anyone had seen anything suspicious, Johnny Mac said. Let it be, the subchief decided. He walked down the dock to turn to making some supper.

FISH, DRUGS, AND DREAMS

A s Ryan and the ranger neared the dock at Bass Harbor, back on Mount Desert Island, the sun was hitting the western horizon. A moist chill crept up from the surface of the water. Losing their solar warmth, the seals sleeping on rocks began slipping back into the sea. The ranger pulled on his forest-green parka. "That's Johnny Mac's work boat there," he said, pointing at a fine forty-footer that was outfitted not just for lobstering but also for tuna and sword-fishing. "And that's his truck—the big black 450." He took a joint from his parka pocket and lit it.

Ryan happened to look over at the ranger and noticed the little brass nameplate his parka bore: GOODWIN. But he didn't ask any questions about the truck or the nameplate. He had something else on his mind.

"What isn't Johnny Mac telling me?" he asked the ranger.

The ranger sighed as he tied up the boat. "Clearly," he said, and took a toke, "he seems to want you to think it was drug business that brought down Ricky Cutts." He let out some of the smoke. "And it might have. I'm no detective, but I'm thinking, what doesn't add up?"

"And," Ryan said, "what doesn't?"

"That meth stash on the boat—you think it would have stayed there that long? Consider the situation. Someone found the boat, brought it around Malpense into the harbor, winched it up on the dry. And it's been sitting there for a few days. Someone stripped the electronics, which takes time and tools. But they didn't take the meth?"

"And?"

"Well, it makes me think he might be decoying you." The ranger waved his hands and did his best imitation of Pee-wee Herman's squeaky voice: "Hey, look at me, I'm a big bad bag of drugs!" Then, back in his own voice, he summarized: "What doesn't he want you to look at? That's what I wonder about."

"And what might that be?"

"I'm wondering about that sturgeon we saw."

"But he takes that legally, at least according to his interpretation," Ryan said. "And the Interior Department isn't going to litigate that now."

"Sure," the ranger replied. "But what does he do with the sturgeon? It's a valuable fish. So is tuna. To some people, more than meth."

"The subchief struck me as pretty honest about his stance. What makes you think different?"

The ranger took another puff. "In the net shed, next to the boat, you saw the big tools—chain saw, gaff hooks, peavey, and such?"

"Yeah?" Ryan was intrigued by them. He'd always liked tools, even if he didn't like the navy.

"Well, one of them, an old sledgehammer, had three old curved blades, probably taken from a bent propeller, welded to each other in distinctive pattern, not just next to each other, but slightly off."

"I saw that," Ryan said. "Figured it was for cutting seaweed or something. Never seen anything like it."

"Nah. It's a specialized item. A tool created in response to federal regulation. We call it a 'prop faker.' You swing those blades a couple few times into the head or back of a sturgeon. Makes it looks like the fish was killed by a boat propeller."

"Why?"

"That's to make it look like what we call a 'vessel strike fish.' Federal regulations say that if you encounter such a fish, you are allowed to keep it."

"Okay," Ryan said. "But why would that be necessary if the tribe maintains that it is legal under the treaty for them to take sturgeon?"

"Because it isn't legal once it is beyond tribal waters—unless it's a vessel strike. And they might eat a few, but they're not going to eat all of it. Too valuable. A big sturgeon can fetch maybe a few thousand dollars. A big bluefin tuna, even more." He examined the end of the joint and then pocketed it in a little metal can. "The prop fake is kind of hokey, because sturgeon are bottom feeders. Still, it makes lacerations, so it offers up an easy excuse for possession."

They walked up the dock. Ryan thanked the ranger for his help. The ranger, as he got into the truck, turned to Ryan with a final thought: "Might be fish. Might be drugs. I don't know the fish market, but on Liberty, for the other, you might want to check in with Abby Buck."

Why him?

"Just ask him about Ricky Cutts. And maybe also about the bag of meth rocks that was on Ricky's boat."

Ryan said he hadn't realized that Abby Buck was involved in drugs. "I just thought he was an entrepreneur, you know, with those Downeast Depots."

"He's pretty canny," the ranger said. "But you just ask him."

Ryan got in his truck and stared at his little yellow dashboard note reminding him. What follow-up questions was he failing to ask today?

Then he checked his messages. The first was something from the lawyers in San Diego. He didn't care and deleted it without listening. Nothing lawyers could do would bring back his wife and children. The second was from a Dorothy Peyton. Ryan didn't recognize the name. Her voicemail said she was the county medical examiner, over in Rockfish, ready to discuss her findings, and that she was "out of town tomorrow, so come on down two days from now." The third was from the administrative assistant in the Baltimore office of the FBI, who said that local databases indicated that a Wanda Cutts had died in a car accident two years ago. There was no indication that she had ever divorced Ricky Cutts.

Driving north to Bangor, Ryan mulled the day's work. *So a law enforcement officer, Johnny Mac, is pointing me toward the drug angle, maybe to keep me from focusing on a fish business connection to a murder? And a park ranger who constantly smokes dope is saying he might be right or might not be?* It felt like he had dropped into an alternate universe. He wanted some music but by mistake turned on the truck's FM radio. National Public Radio news came on, with its soft but urgent tones. Something was happening with the Federal Reserve Board and inflation. He hadn't listened to the news for months. He hit the right button for his own music, from his phone to the truck's speakers via Bluetooth.

He thought about the stoned ranger as he listened to Hank Williams's greatest hits, the only music he had played since the accident. *The ranger's family name is Goodwin? Really, the same as Caleb's? For Chrissake,* he thought to himself as he drove through the lonesome streets of Bangor. He made a mental note to ask Caleb about that. *What else am I missing?* he wondered. He was painfully conscious that as an investigator, he had lost a step. He let out a long sigh. What was it that Warren Buffet had once said? "If you've been playing poker for half an hour and you don't know who the patsy at the table is—well, then, you're the patsy."

At home he sat at his laptop and scrolled through the various treaties held by the Indians of Maine—a word that some preferred, even until this day, to "Native Americans" or the Canadians' "First Peoples." According to several tribes' interpretation, the state remained bound by pacts signed between them and the Massachusetts Bay Colony, some going back to the seventeenth century—that is, predating the creation of the United States. He read that in the 1820 treaty renegotiations, the lead tribal negotiator, a Penobscot named John Neptune, had lambasted the Whites' mishandling of deer herds, saying they shot too many young ones. Also, he complained, their mill dams were interfering with the annual upriver migration of salmon and alewives. The state then agreed to pay an annual compensation package to the tribes of five hundred bushels of corn, fifteen barrels of good flour, one hundred yards of broadcloth (red one year, blue the next, the treaty specified), one hundred pounds of gunpowder, four hundred pounds of shot, one hundred fifty pounds of tobacco, six boxes of chocolate, and fifty dollars in silver.

Fatigued from the day's trip to Malpense, and especially from the odd tension with the subchief, he went to bed early without eating. On this night he had a new dream. He was in the back seat of their SUV during the crash. The frantic slowing of time as his wife swung the wheel left. The kids screaming. Then just a black curtain. He awoke drenched in sweat at 3:00 A.M., with his fingers clenched and his nails digging into his palms. He drank a coffee on the back porch and watched the moon. He heard the low unhurried call of an owl—*who who who whooo*. He wondered if it was the one that had swooped him on his run.

He showered, dressed, and headed for Liberty. Still the nightmare clung to him like a shroud as he drove south. He remembered the day, two months after the crash, when Wundermin, his supervisor at the FBI's San Diego field office, came to his house and asked Ryan about his plans. Ryan, sitting in his Tilt-A-Whirl armchair, as he thought of it, asked to be assigned as far from San Diego as possible.

"Like, Alaska?" Wundermin replied. He sounded dubious.

"Farther," Ryan said. "Maine."

Wundermin asked if Ryan was sure of that. Ryan said he was. Wundermin said, "Ryan, you're no waterwalker. But you're a dependable agent with a good future. You show up on time, and you get the job done. Why throw it away?"

"I don't think I am the man I used to be," Ryan confessed. The old Ryan, that calm, steady, somewhat predictable man, had been shattered. The new one would need to start over, somewhere else. He did not disclose to his boss his fear that he no longer had all his brainpower. But he suspected that Wundermin sensed it. Since the accident, some part of Ryan's mind had been occupied by death and darkness, sapping his abilities to observe and analyze. He estimated to himself that he was operating at about 80 percent of his old capacity. And back then he had been just a middling FBI agent. So what was he now? He wasn't sure.

"Okay," said Wundermin. He shrugged. He had tried. But he was no miracle worker. A good manager, he believed, did what he could and then moved on to the next problem. Ryan was damaged goods and was about to become some other manager's problem.

SCRIPTURE READING

I t was Sunday. Ryan decided to head down to Liberty Island to attend the services at the Congregational church. It was 220 years old, small, white, and plain. It had the pleasant fragrance of well-aged wood, from its great thick rafters down to its bare floor, which was a kind of lumber not available anymore, maple planks some fourteen or fifteen inches wide, and probably two or three inches thick. This was a house built to last.

It was the first time he had been in a church since the triple funeral after the accident. He barely had memories of that ceremony, just disjointed images of people crying, people singing, himself weeping, sobbing. And his dry-eyed father, as detached as always, awkwardly patting him on the back as he bent forward in physical grief, muttering under his breath, "C'mon, Ryan," as if losing your family were like losing a touch football game.

As the bell tolled eleven o'clock, he settled in a rear pew, made of bare, undecorated brown wood like all of them. The summer people had yet to arrive on the island, so there were only about forty worshippers, most of them gathered near the front rows. He felt relief in the Congregationalists' old-school approach. First, the call to worship. "Happy we are," a reader said. The churchgoers responded, "When our pain is held in the balm of love." The words zoomed into Ryan's skull. Then a few turgid hymns, marching along in rigid four-four time, sounding almost like chants.

A parishioner arose and walked up to the pulpit to read from scripture. Ryan recognized him—it was Herc, the Highliner who sat next to Caleb at the Fisherman's Pal. Herc looked out over the congregation without introducing himself, which of course was unnecessary as he was speaking before people who had known him all his life. He was hatless, being in church, and Ryan saw that Herc had crew cut blond hair, and a forehead that was almost white, in contrast to his sunbrowned cheeks and arms. He said, simply, "Luke 17." The lobsterman read slowly and gravely, like a judge delivering a sentence: "It were better for him that a millstone were hanged about his neck, and he cast into the sea, than that he should offend one of these little ones. Take heed to yourselves: if thy brother trespass against thee, rebuke him; and if he repent, forgive him." Ryan weighed the words and, looking around, decided that these islanders took Bible passages about fishermen and the sea quite seriously.

Ryan was surprised the sermon was titled "Jesus Was a Refugee." When the female minister stepped up to the pulpit, he noticed that one of the older men in front of him removed his hearing aid. Others closed their eyes. They had known what was coming: the minister delivered an almost radical message, that the refugees coming to the United States were the meek and the poor, and that God would know who had shunned or harassed them, and those who were guilty of that one day would face a sorely disappointed deity. They would be, she promised, "sinners in the hands of an angry God." When she finished, the man replaced his hearing aid.

Then came the Lord's Prayer and the doxology, both voiced in a low rumble by all those present: "Praise God, from who all blessings flow."

It was a pleasant and consoling way to pass a weekend hour. Ryan felt a ray of gratitude for those words of wisdom—"pain held in the balm of love." It had been a long time since he had felt thankful for anything.

The minister opened her arms high and, with her white robes fluttering, encouraged them to go in peace. The doors of the church opened. Like most people, Ryan needed a moment, after the stately and low-key church service, to adjust back to the bustle and noise of the real world. He stood in the morning sunlight and looked around. Herc nodded hello.

"That was a good reading," Ryan said. "Did you select it?"

"No, I'm not that smart," Herc said, but clearly pleased that Ryan had heard him speak. "That was emailed to me by the deacons."

Ryan was unfamiliar with the church's organization and must have looked puzzled, because Herc went on to explain, "The deacons, they're the ones who run the church. The minister, well, she's a nice lady from away, put it that way. She visits the sick and organizes the services. The old folks like that." Herc held out his left arm. "And here's one of our deacons," he said, gesturing toward the tall, sunburned man standing next to him. "Agent Tapia, this is Topsail Pennyman. He fishes the grounds just west of where Ricky's area was." By now, Ryan was no longer surprised by the unusual names on the island, but even this one struck him as a rarity.

"Did you work with Ricky Cutts much?" Ryan asked.

"No, we didn't cross paths a lot," Topsail said. "We each had our own grounds. But if he needed help, he'd generally head the other way, over to the Malpense dock." And, Topsail thought, sometimes Ricky would go over to Malpense for other reasons. "Never had trouble with him," Topsail added. Ryan got the message that Topsail hadn't gone out of his way to visit with Ricky.

Topsail had a question of his own: "Have you talked to Ricky's mother?"

Ryan was surprised. "No, no one's mentioned her," he said. "She's still alive?"

"Well," Topsail said, "she's kinda lost it. Up in the hospital in Bangor. The one for, you know, crazy people. Still, she might have something to say."

"Thanks, I'll look into it," Ryan said.

Topsail turned to Herc and said, "Liked the way you read the scripture today. Hit me in the gut."

OTHER GOVERNMENT AGENCY

R yan decided to drive back to Ricky Cutts's house, now that he had a bit better understanding of the man, to see if he noticed anything more on a second try. It was one of those small disciplines of investigation. You wonder why you are doing it, but you never know what might turn up. This time he concentrated on the outside. The backyard was now filled by the four hundred traps of Ricky's that the lobstermen of Liberty Island had collected and stacked out there. He walked around the traps, but nothing unusual presented itself to his untrained eye. He moved to the front and walked its perimeter. Then again, another tighter loop. He wasn't looking for clues to the crime as much as clues to the man. What had led to his dismal end? But nothing caught his eye, just the rusty residue of a trashy life.

He was sitting in his truck, thinking about his next move, when he saw a black Mercedes two-door coupe come down the paved road and turn onto a dirt driveway that led into the woods. This would be Ricky's closest neighbor, he realized, and so might be worth talking to. But in the same moment, he thought that driving that expensive vehicle in Maine, with just one interstate highway and many smaller roads potholed by long winters and pavement heavily salted for months at a time, seemed kind of a waste.

He waited a few minutes, then headed down the driveway the Mercedes had taken, so deeply graveled that anyone entering would have to drive slowly and would be noisy. It curved downhill through thick fir and spruce stands a quarter mile to a house on the coast. This place was the diametric opposite of Ricky Cutts's forlorn abode. It was a high-style New England "cottage," two stories, with unpainted wooden shingles and green trim. Lilacs bloomed in the dooryard. Standing hidden away, far from the road, it seemed to state that it was owned by old money that didn't wish to be noticed.

He knocked, and soon the door was opened by a white-haired man in his seventies dressed like an aging Oxford professor—thick, baggy wide-wale tan corduroys; a black-and-blue tattersall-patterned shirt; a blue silk bow tie; and an old red wool sweater vest. A pair of glasses hung from his neck on a librarian's chain. He had the air of a formal man dressed in what he considered his informal attire. He had not expected a visitor. "Yes?" he said. And waited, holding the door.

Ryan stood on the steps and explained that he was a federal agent conducting an investigation and would like to ask a few questions about a neighbor. "Ah, the FBI man," he said. "Doing a preemployment background check on someone, I suppose? Very well, every job has its moments of drudgery." Ryan wondered if he was correct in detecting a dollop of condescension in the man's voice.

Rather than invite Ryan in, the man stood squarely in the doorway and asked to see some credentials. Ryan handed over the leather wallet that held his badge and driver's license. The man took each from its sheath and read them with thoroughness. He looked up once as if he were an immigration officer comparing the photo to Ryan's face. Then, unusually, he took them from the holder and turned them over to look at the obverse sides, for reasons that Ryan could not discern.

"Based in Bangor, eh?" the man said.

Ryan said nothing.

"Sorry," the man drawled, slowly handing back the IDs, in a tone that was far from apologetic. "Old training kicks in." He explained he had worked for "another government agency"—a phrase Ryan knew from his training time at the FBI Academy in Quantico as the insiders' too cute, barely disguised term for the CIA. He invited Ryan to sit on the living room couch. Ryan walked across a huge Persian carpet, a black border surrounding a complex ruby-red interior, and sat at the end of couch. At his elbow stood an elaborate, tall, slender coffeepot with a coned top of filigreed silver. Ryan glanced at it. "From Yemen, home of coffee," the man informed him, moving in a slow, almost stately manner. But he did not offer Ryan coffee or tea, nor even a glass of water.

The far end of the room was dominated by a Grotrian G-165 piano, a make known for its precision and responsiveness, sitting next to a picture window overlooking the ocean, with several green islands scattered in the sunny distance. Just down the hill, Ryan could see a sailboat. It was a green-hulled wooden Herreshoff 12 ½, the sailing equivalent of the little Mercedes and the baby grand, bobbed at the dock below. These were the trophies of a man who valued well-crafted, expensive objects—especially small, fast ones.

The man settled into a tall rocking chair that positioned him to gaze down at Ryan. He said nothing.

"Where did you serve?" Ryan asked.

"I finished up in Rabat," he said. He allowed that he had been station chief there, showing Ryan that he had once held high rank in the agency. Ryan guessed that was a reward tour for a career spent largely in the Middle East—Cairo, Baghdad, Damascus, Oman, Riyadh, something like that. Now, in retirement, the man said, his days were preoccupied by translating a medieval Arab historian from Granada who he thought should be better known. Ryan caught the implication, somehow, that the man doubted Ryan spoke any foreign languages worth knowing. With that thought Ryan caught himself—in just a few moments, this guy had gotten on his nerves, which was the wrong posture for an investigator.

Seeing where Ryan was looking, the man said, "On summer afternoons I sail out among those islands. I find that Penobscot Bay in August is utter peace, almost the opposite of my time in the Middle East." He gestured at the sailboat. "A nimble craft, probably the best sailboat ever designed. Certainly one of the prettiest." He looked at Ryan. "Do you sail?" he asked.

"Only a Hobie Cat," Ryan replied, reaching back to his early days in San Diego as a bachelor.

The man almost recoiled at the mention of a boat he considered a plastic beach toy. "Ah, quite unfit for these cold, foggy waters," the man intoned. "Even a mite dangerous, I'd say." He made it sound like Ryan had personally offended him.

All in all, this man had done his best to demonstrate to Ryan that the FBI man was out of his depth and severely outclassed. But why? Ryan had given no indication of his mission.

"So, how can I help you?" the man said.

"Well, first," Ryan said, "what's your name?"

The man frowned. "Wouldn't a minimally competent agent know that before he let his knuckles hit my door?" he said.

Ryan considered that. This guy was on the attack. But why?

The CIA man went in another direction. "I suspect that right now you are wondering how someone who was a career federal employee can afford this house, that car, that boat, this carpet, that piano? 'Did he fiddle his expense accounts for decades, or inherit or marry wealth? And just where is that wife, anyway?'"

"If you say so," Ryan said. "What's the story?"

"Those questions are inappropriate, because they are irrelevant to the subject of your investigation," the man parried.

"Which you think is?"

"Which, rather, I know is the violent death of my neighbor, Ricky Cutts," the man said. "Your presence is the unfortunate consequence of jurisdictional problems that have thrust you into a situation about which you know little and are likely to do more damage than good."

Ryan had had enough. He stared at the man. "Why are you being this way?" he finally asked. "Is it hazing an outsider? Or some interagency feud of yours?"

"You are correct; I have never liked the FBI," he said. "When they were on my turf, your people tended to foul things up, seeing the world in black-and-white, and always in the short term, always looking for an arrest, never taking the long view, about what a good outcome would be. Also, in my view, they tended to elevate their bureau's interest above the national interest. So, yes," he admitted, "I've never liked your shop." Ryan noticed the man's use of British intelligence jargon, another snobbish reminder of the differences between the CIA and the FBI.

"Also, more specifically, early in my career, in the guise of being a Canadian academic researcher, I was in Algeria and interviewed some of the Black Panthers who had fled there. I must say I found their accounts of the FBI's murderous and illegal campaign against the Panthers to be quite compelling.

"So no," he concluded, rocking back and forth slowly, "you people don't have a lot of credibility with me."

Ryan chuckled at the gall of the man. "Like you guys didn't shoot people in the back at night without warning?"

"Not American citizens," the man retorted. He thought to himself, *At least not before 9/11.*

"At any rate," Ryan persisted, "I don't think all that has anything remotely to do with my current inquiry."

The man in turn rocked his chair forward and stopped, planting his feet and leaning forward. "Oh, but it does, it does, little grass-hopper," he said. He waited for Ryan to catch up. Ryan had the feeling of being played with, like a fish on a line.

"How?" Ryan asked.

Ryan would have to wait for that. The hook was set. The man reached for a meerschaum pipe on the end table, packed it with Latakia tobacco, lit it, and waited. He waved out the match, then inhaled and expressed a long puff of smoke into the space between them. "You, Mr. Tapia, were taught to track down bad guys," he began. "For you, an arrest means success." But, he continued, pro-fessorially, "That is merely a tactical outcome. By which I mean, the world doesn't end when your case ends. So by your very training, you neglect the more important issue: How does your action change the world? That is the strategic issue. It always is."

Ryan didn't like the pompous lecturing, but he had been taught at the academy that once a person being questioned begins talking, you don't try to stop them. "So," he asked, "if you were my super-visor, what would you recommend be my course of action?"

The man sighed. "Where to begin? First, I would tell you, young man, to pull up your socks. You seem a bit, uh, at loose ends. Get your act together, as they say.

"Once you can execute the basics, then—were I your overseer—I would instruct you to examine where you are now. Literally con-sider the ground on which you stand. There is a vast difference between the FBI's view of the world and the islanders' view. That tension, made manifest by your presence on the island, already is disturbing its ecology." He let out another big puff of tobacco smoke and watched it dissipate above Ryan's head. "My family has been summering in these islands for over a century, yet we are still outsiders. That's all right. We understand that. It is a beautiful place but a fragile one."

"So my next step is?" Ryan asked.

"End it," the man said. "Nothing good can come of your investigation. Do what the local law enforcement agencies do: let the natives handle it."

Ryan tried again. "What can you tell me about Ricky Cutts?"

The man sighed. "I have nothing for you on that. And now I want to get back to my work." He put a hand on either arm of the rocking chair and stood, showing that in his view, the interview was finished. But he made no move to escort Ryan out.

Ryan walked himself to the door. As he gently closed it, he heard a single crashing chord on the piano. Had he known classical music, he would have recognized it as the subito opening in C minor of Beethoven's *Pathétique* sonata. The man was playing a musical pun on Ryan's investigation.

Back in the truck, Ryan drove out to the main road. Then he pulled over and looked up the name of the rude retired spy. According to Maine state records, the house was occupied and the Mercedes was owned by a Samuel Bissell. He thought about the CIA man's language, the British tinge to it, his use of the words "overseer," "natives," and "turf." *That probably had been the man's attitude and advice in various Middle Eastern countries,* he thought.

He was hot and ill at ease, almost as if Bissell had slapped him. Ryan knew he was not working at his best, but this was the first time someone had called him on it. He pointed the truck northward toward Bangor. He wondered just how sloppy he had become. It had been quite a Sunday. Hank Williams was singing away, rotating through the usual thirty-four tunes. But today the song that caught Ryan's ear was one in which old Hank asked, "Why doncha mind your own business?" *Not quite a theme song for a struggling FBI man*, Ryan discontentedly thought.

Back home, he sat on the back porch and googled Bissell but found little about the man's career. But the name popped up in some histories of Maine that he found online. He spent hours poring through them. This in turn led him to the digitized version of pension records of Revolutionary War soldiers from the district of Maine in the state of Massachusetts. There he found a Topsail Pennyman who in fact had been a sergeant. He guessed that what had begun as a nickname had become a family tradition, passed downward from one generation to the next. In the same records, he found Goodwins, Fernalds, and Bucks. He was about to close his laptop when it occurred to him to look up one more name. Indeed, he soon saw several Cutts also had been soldiers from Maine in the Revolution.

He emerged from his dive into state history feeling the need for a run. It was night now, and a heavy cloud cover obscured the moon and night sky, making it darker than usual. Ryan jogged slowly to the paved road, then turned around. A minute later he nearly tripped over a black bear out for an evening stroll. The bear, about the size and color of a plump Labrador retriever, didn't seem offended or even much alarmed, and just changed course and trotted into the woods. Ryan realized the animals in these woods hadn't had much human company lately. Nor had he.

MEETING THE TOWN MANAGER

A t 5:00 A.M. on Monday, Ryan was back on the Liberty commercial wharf. He asked Caleb about the high-end fish business hereabouts.

"Isn't really a market, just one lady over in Rockfish," Caleb said.

That was convenient, Ryan thought. He was heading there soon to see the medical examiner. While there, he could learn more about the sturgeon trade. "What's that woman's name?"

"Over to Rockfish? She's Solid Harrison."

"Sally?" Ryan asked, not catching the name.

"No," Caleb replied. "'Solid,' like rock-solid."

"Some kind of island name?"

"Hell no," Caleb laughed. "Parents were back-to-the-earth hippies. Named her Solidarity. She has a business, Top Shelf, at the southern end of the Rockfish docks."

Abby Buck walked by, on his way into the Fisherman's Pal. "Morning, Caleb," he said quietly. But the lobsterman only raised a chin in acknowledgment. Ryan noticed the cold vibe between the two, but didn't know what to make of it. Maybe it was just two different worlds, he thought—one a man of business, the other a man of the sea.

After breakfast at the Pal—coffee and a pecan roll, in his case—
Ryan walked back to his truck, where he called Solid Harrison to
request a meeting. She was agreeable. "Why don't you come by
after you see the medical examiner?"

Ryan actually stared at his cell phone for a moment. A quick
thought crossed his mind: *Is someone listening in on my calls?*

Solid Harrison was a step ahead of him. "Don't be so paranoid,"
she pooh-poohed. "Maine is a small place. Dorothy is my partner.
I know you're seeing her on Tuesday."

He also made an appointment to see Mrs. Shirley Cutts, who,
as Topsail had indicated, resided in the state psychiatric hospital
on the northern outskirts of Bangor.

His last step was to check his messages. The latest one was from
the town manager, who said he would like to meet Ryan. The town
office was visible just outside the windshield, so Ryan hopped out
and walked over. He introduced himself to the clerk at the front
desk, who was the woman who handled boat registrations—a major
source of the town's revenue, after real estate taxes.

The manager heard him and strolled out, a man perhaps in his
late fifties, wearing khakis and a brown cardigan sweater that had
a homemade look. He was balding and wore glasses and a well-
trimmed moustache. "I'm Freddy Ghent," he said, extending his
hand. "I hear you're doing some work here and just wanted to see
if I could lend a hand."

Hmm, Ryan thought. A small warning bell rang in the back of
his head.

They sat. Behind the manager's head, a handwritten sign was
thumbtacked to the wall: SWRS. Ryan asked what it meant. Ghent
said, "Snowplowing, Water, Roads, Sewers—the four pillars of my
job. Most of the people who come in here, I point to the sign and
say, 'Which one?' But I am guessing that's not the case with you."

After small talk about how long he had been in Maine and so on, Freddy's brow wrinkled, and he tugged on the end of his moustache a bit. These were his signals that he was going into his serious mode. "You know, friend, your poking around has upset some people."

Ryan found the usage of "friend" strange, especially on Liberty. This guy clearly was not an islander. Except for the balding head, Freddy Ghent reminded Ryan of the Ned Flanders character on *The Simpsons*. *What was Flanders's job in that show?* he wondered. *Perhaps he was the Springfield town manager.*

"Bothering anyone in particular?" Ryan asked mildly.

"No," the town manager said, "just generally, knocking around the island. I'll be in the grocery store, or gassing up my car, and people say something at me, 'What's going on with this Ricky Cutts thing, how come his death warrants a federal investigation?' 'Ricky was nothing special,' one guy said to me. People don't like it. Makes them uneasy."

Ghent didn't say it, but the town needed to maintain its image as a quaint and cozy destination where tourists might witness the real Maine of simple people wresting their living from the sea and the land. Talk of a body bobbing in the seaweed didn't help that effort. Nor did rumors the town manager was hearing about the FBI agent asking questions about drugs.

"It's unfortunate," Ryan said, "but the jurisdiction situation landed the case on my desk."

"I get that," the manager said. "Boy howdy, I do. Sorting out jurisdictions takes up a lot of my time in this job, between roads, schools, aid to education, aid to the elderly, different state and federal regulators for the environment and such. Town, county, state, federal, even got some issues with Canada, their lobsters trucked down here and ours going up, depending on the price differential between over the border and here."

He shifted gears a bit. "Look, I know these island people can seem a little unfriendly. Hell, I moved up here from Gorland, looking for a quieter pace, and it took some people a year to say hello, just recognize my presence.

"But it really is a good little town. We want to do right by you. You look like you could use a workspace. You can have the meeting room at the top floor of the town library, just down the way. It's unused pretty much all the time, except Monday nights, when the Alcoholics Anonymous people meet there. You'd have to leave then, unless of course you're a member."

"Thanks, but I do most of my work from my truck," Ryan said. "Is there anything else on your mind?"

"No," Ghent said. "I just hope you can wind up this investigation thing soon."

"So do I," Ryan replied. He stood.

They walked together past the clerk and toward the front door of the town office. Ryan knew this point, at the farewell, was often when people delivered the message they really wanted to send. And Freddy Ghent struck him as the most predictable of men. So he wasn't surprised when Ghent drew himself up at the door and said, "You know, when the selectmen interviewed me for this job, they only asked one question."

"What was that?"

"They said, 'How would you fix this town?'"

"And?" Ryan asked.

"It was a trick question," the manager replied. "They posed it to try to determine if I would come in aiming to change the place, to make it more like Gorland or other towns on the mainland."

"So what did you say?"

"I told them I wasn't here to 'fix' anything, that I wanted to help Liberty Island be Liberty Island. That the job, as I understood it, was to discern the wishes of the town and help those wishes be fulfilled."

"And so they hired you?"

"Yep," he said. He extended his hand and wished Ryan "good luck in wrapping up this thing, so the town can relax."

Still shaking hands, Ryan smiled and said, "What do you think of Abby Buck?" He was tired of being played with.

Ghent's hand shot backward, as if an electric shock had hit it. His tone changed entirely. "Why do you ask?" he said coldly.

"Just wondering. People say things."

Ghent drew himself up indignantly. "Abby Buck has never been charged with anything," he said. "To the best of my knowledge, he is a successful businessman who employs several people on the island and supports local charities. And speaking of things people say, I hear you have to screw up pretty badly in the FBI to get shipped to Bangor. Or be screwed up by something." The town manager looked Ryan squarely in the eye. "When outsiders come to rural Maine, it's usually because they're looking for a second chance, or a new start. No one comes here without a reason." With that he carefully and slowly closed the front door of the town office.

That was the message from the manager, Ryan thought as he walked back to his truck. *Get this thing finished, and get off the island.* He mused to himself that it used to be the job of the police to say, "Move along, nothing to see here." But then there was no police force on Liberty Island.

With Ryan gone, the town manager walked back into his office, slammed its own door, and looked out his window at Ryan getting into his truck. Ghent muttered under his breath, "Asshole." He barely was able to work the rest of the day. Instead he stared at the ceiling and reviewed again and again the series of unfortunate events that had led him to this dead end on the ragged edge of the Maine coast.

THE MORAL JUDGMENTS OF A DRUG DEALER

From the cab of the truck, Ryan dialed Abby Buck's number. He needed to see this guy again. In their earlier meeting, at the Fisherman's Pal, Ryan had no sense that Abby Buck was involved in drugs. All that Ryan had known then was that when he had knocked on the front door of Sarah's Shelter, the woman there had told him to go talk to the guy.

Buck picked up on the first ring. "Agent Tapia?" he said. Ryan wasn't sure how Buck had caller ID'd him, but he got the implied message that Buck was on the ball. He gave Ryan the address. Ryan drove over and saw a mobile home with lobster traps out front. As he turned into the driveway, Ryan thought it could be any home on Liberty. But he noticed two anomalies. One was an unusual addition that distinguished it from a typical house on the island: it had a tall, long white fence running across the entire front yard, obscuring from public view just who might be parking in Buck's driveway. And there were at least a dozen cameras and motion detectors perched in the trees. Buck could sit inside and see anyone within five hundred yards of his house.

As he approached, the door of the mobile home swung open. Buck wore blue jeans and a Patriots hoodie. *The drug dealer relaxing at home*, Ryan thought. What surprised Ryan is that Buck was not at all furtive. He acted like he had the upper hand.

And perhaps he did. Within a few minutes, Ryan had the eerie sense that this guy knew the island's secrets, even some that many islanders barely suspected. Where the bodies were, and where the narcotics were stashed. Who was using. Whose kid was heading for trouble. Who was desperate for cash.

The entrepreneurial Mr. Buck's manner with him was mild, even tranquil. He showed no anxiety about the FBI man's visit. "I know why you're here, and it ain't about my businesses," he said at the outset.

"Your businesses are, uh, more widespread than our previous talk led me to understand," Ryan said. He didn't know quite how to broach the subject.

Buck decided he would make it easy for Ryan. "All right. Straight up: one of my businesses is providing some drugs on the island—oxy and stuff," he said. No more, no less, and no apologies. Just a statement of fact. "If that was the problem that had interested the feds," he said, "it would be the DEA knocking on my door, not an FBI guy.

"Look," he said straightforwardly, "I make my money by providing services. That's one of them." He opened a bottle of craft IPA and offered it to Ryan, who shook his head.

Ryan found the man's ease astonishing. He spoke as if he enjoyed immunity—and perhaps he did. Normally Ryan would stay on topic, but sheer curiosity provoked him to ask, "Why do the people here put up with you? How do you survive, with what happened to that dealer from near Boston, killed in his Cadillac?"

"You don't get it," Buck said, with a slight smile. "I had nothing to do with that. The island did that guy, that Mitch from Revere Beach. He was low-end. Opposite of me. He sold bad coke to some kids who took it to the prom after-party last year, down on the beach. It had a shitload of fentanyl in it. Killed three kids that night, including a cousin of mine." In a high school with a graduating class of just sixteen, the loss of those three teenagers was a catastrophe, an unrepairable hole in the life of the island.

"But the island is okay with you?"

"Yeah," he said and sipped his beer.

"Why?"

"They know me. And I know them." The Bucks had been on the island since the American Revolution, he said. "More important, I know the rules. I don't sell to kids. In fact, I've called a minister, told him confidentially that his son, maybe fifteen years old, was asking me to sell him some coke, he needed to watch the kid, talk to him. Just a quiet heads-up.

"Like I told you, I'm an entrepreneur. I'm not flashy. Mitch showed up on the island in a Caddy, which is like a flashing neon sign to people around here. I keep my head down. I drive an old Camry. I'm a dependable supporter of local charities. I don't get violent. Someone on the island gets hurt on the job, I contribute to the health care fund—and without making a big thing about it.

"And most of all, I provide something they want. Everyone needs two things to work out on the water: fuel and bait. Some guys need a third: dope. Maybe oxy, maybe just codeine for your legs and back. Maybe some grass to pass the hours afloat. And some heroin for the downtime." He saw himself as just another supplier. "Dope has always followed the fishing trade, and always will, until robots take it over. And maybe even after then."

Buck moved on to his summary of what he wanted Ryan to understand. "So the question the island faces is not what you think.

It is not, 'Should drugs be sold here?' It is, 'What kind of person will we allow to sell drugs here?'

"The island is at peace with me," he said. "I'm a known quantity, not a stranger, and I'm selling clean stuff at decent prices to the right people. With no gunplay."

"Well then," Ryan asked, "why doesn't Caleb Goodwin seem to think much of you?"

Buck was taken aback. His eyes flashed at Ryan. "Did he say something about me?" he asked quickly.

"No, no, no," Ryan assured the drug dealer. "Nothing like that. I was just noticing the way you two seemed kind of distant with each other yesterday."

Buck looked pained. "Yeah, I saw that too. He thinks he's so high and mighty. And I'm some kind of insect to be tolerated. But bottom line is, he's just a businessman, and so am I."

Ryan nodded. "As part of your business, did you sell to Ricky Cutts?"

"Of course," Buck said. "The gas station doesn't turn away customers it doesn't like. Neither do I."

"With Cutts, what kind, in what amounts?"

"Mainly meth, some coke, in what I think of as 'seller-user' quantities—that is, someone looking to sell enough drugs to cover his own usage."

Ryan waited a beat. "But?"

But yeah. "He was a shit, a very low human being," Buck said.

Ryan found that moral judgment rich, coming from a drug dealer. He kept that opinion to himself. "How so?" he inquired. But, as everyone kept telling him, the world looked different from the island.

"He was a dirty guy. I heard bad things about him."

"Like what? Did he cross the Malpenses? Mess with other fishermen? Something else?"

"Not for me to say," Buck said, not even bothering to state the obvious: he was not going to share the island's secrets with an outsider, most especially a lawman from somewhere far away. "You'd have to ask them."

Buck walked Ryan to the pickup. There he had a final word for him: "By the way, I don't sell to the Malpense. But I hear he did."

TRIBAL TOES AND BOAT WAKES

B ack in the truck, Ryan saw a "CALL ME URGENT" text from Harriet in Portland. When he was off the island, he pulled over into a primitive rest stop, really just a few parking spaces on a dirt pullout on the side of the road with a big green steel trash can.

She cut to the chase. "Do I need to ask you to come down to Portland for a meeting?" she said.

"What's up?" Ryan asked.

She had been up to Augusta the previous day for a federal-state-local enforcement hoedown. Usually those were just meet-and-greet exercises, but they were worthwhile because you should get to know your counterparts before a crisis hits, and also because sometimes you learned about new resources or trends. "So I'm getting a coffee, and a guy dumping sugar in his cup turns out to be the Washington County sheriff, glances at my name tag, and says, 'Oh, you're the guys that are stepping on tribal toes in my territory.'"

She waited, as if she had asked a question. "Probably just the sheriff showing that nothing happens on his turf without him knowing," Ryan replied.

"Maybe so, but tread carefully," Harriet said. "I mean, we're still living down some of the shakeout from Wounded Knee, back in 1973," she added.

He knew that she was doing her job, which was to protect the FBI as much as it was to manage him, but he was still irked by what seemed to him to be second-guessing.

"Keep me posted, and don't take a step against a member of the tribe without running it by me first," she ordered.

"Of course," he said, recalling to himself that he had been told that Harriet's nickname in the bureau was Harriet the Harrier, after the marine jet that could fly low and hover.

A great fatigue washed over Ryan after that call. He reached behind the seat and pulled out the winter coat he kept there. He watched a chickadee feeding. It flew to a berried bush, pecked three times, then departed. A minute later it reappeared for three more pecks. Ryan admired the tough little bird, which seemed to him to capture the essence of the Maine woods. Chickadees, he had noticed, were almost always the first species to locate a food source. But they never lingered, as sparrows and doves do, eating for several minutes without moving much. It was late afternoon when he closed his eyes.

It was 4:00 A.M. when he awoke. He looked around the quiet rest stop. For some reason he had slept solidly, leaning against the driver's window of the truck, for almost eleven hours. He drove out of the rest stop in the early dawn to the Fisherman's Pal, had a cup of coffee and a roll, but did not see Caleb. So he walked over to the commercial wharf.

"Been out to Malpense, eh?" Caleb greeted him with a grin. Ryan was no longer taken aback that everyone seemed to know his business.

But it still hurt to feel like he was the last to know anything. "Walk with me," he said. Then he asked, "You don't like Abby Buck much, do you?" He was thinking of the cold shoulders he had seen them give each other.

Caleb slowed his pace and made that elaborate frown that one pulls when mulling how to respond to a hard question. "No," he said in a slow, measured tone, "not really. He's a slick talker, that one. I understand he plays a role. Not one I like."

"Is there more?" Ryan asked, and waited.

Caleb frowned. "I guess so. What gripes me is this: I get this sense that he thinks he's the future and I'm the past. And what really gets me is, I suspect he might be right. He has it figured out. I don't. So, you know, he's thinks he's the smart money, and I'm the dummy out there making my living the old-fashioned way, freezing my ass off half the year." Yet it remained clear to Ryan that, given the choice, Caleb would far rather be himself than be Abby Buck. "Freezing my ass off" was as much boasting as complaining. Caleb walked in the steps of his fathers. Abby did not, unless perhaps his forebears were moonshiners.

"But you still don't think he killed Ricky Cutts?"

"No," Caleb said and stopped walking to focus on what he was saying, and on the person he was saying it to. "I don't. He's too smart for that. There was no money in coming down on Ricky Cutts. And Abby is all about the greenbacks. As he will tell you. I understand that. But I don't have to like it." He resumed walking. Ryan left him at the *Sea Angel*, tied up at a prime spot at the end of the wharf.

Back home in Bangor, Ryan opened his laptop and found the federal site for nautical charts. He went to the chart for the area between Liberty Island and Malpense Island. It was dotted with dozens of small islands, like Big Bold, and hundreds of rock outcroppings, which tended to be named by mariners for their appearance—Brown Cow, Whale's Back, Roaring Bull, Black

Horse, White Horse. His eye tracked southeast across the chart to Ricky Cutts's fishing ground, where the murder likely had occurred, a bit to the west of Malpense Island. North of that, the chart showed a long depth in the water, where it plunged to over four hundred feet, called Champlain's Hole, probably a gouge in the sea bottom made during the age when mile-thick glaciers carved the bedrock here.

He switched over to Google Maps and called up the satellite imagery of Champlain's Hole. It stood out as a deeper blue than the surrounding waters. He looked farther to the west and saw that the satellite had caught the curving wake of a boat. He zoomed in. He could clearly see the white paint on the foredeck and main deck but couldn't tell whose boat it actually was. *A seasoned eye probably could*, he thought. He went to the FBI's database and found more imagery. There was the same boat again. It was, he decided, probably Ricky Cutts's *Pussy Man*.

Then he sat on the back porch and opened the little book Wundermin had sent. He read it without a break for two hours, when he was chilled by the long wailing cry of a loon on the pond. His takeaway from the book was that a person should find ways to focus on life, on the living, no matter how small or insignificant. Running helped a bit. He jogged out to the paved road and back. This time, no wildlife visited him.

Then came another night of bad dreams. Trying to sleep was a chore. Wundermin's slim book seemed to have no advice on that.

ASYLUM

R yan skipped breakfast, as had become his habit. After two cups
of coffee on the back porch, his work day began at the state
insane asylum on the northern outskirts of Bangor. It was a huddle
of old brick buildings, three and four stories, with mansard roofs
covered in black slate and a dozen high, thin chimneys, indicating
it was built before central heating was common. It looked like
something out of a Stephen King novel, Ryan thought as he parked.
That made sense, he thought, because that hugely popular horror
author was the town's most famous resident.

The assistant superintendent for women led him to a conference
room off the lobby. "She was involuntarily committed by a state
court," the warden said, as if in warning. "She is not considered
cooperative." Yet when told that a federal investigator wanted to
speak with her, Mrs. Cutts had agreed, she said.

The old woman was brought in by an attendant. She took a chair
at the conference table opposite him, but sat down there sideways to
the table, looking almost over her shoulder at him. The records
stated she was sixty-five years old, but she looked three decades older
than that, almost ancient. She was emaciated, all over. Thin, greasy
gray hair. The skin of her small hands seemed almost translucent.

She wore green hospital pajamas. Over that she wore an old red parka. Over that she had draped a tan nylon hospital blanket, pulling it around her shoulders as she hunched forward. Even though the room was warm, she still looked cold. The attendant stood against the wall a few feet behind her.

Ryan introduced himself.

"Cigarette," she responded quietly. It wasn't a request; it was a demand.

Ryan looked to the warden, who nodded to the attendant, who returned with the requested item. Shirley Cutts lit it and pulled on it eagerly, burning a bit of it down with each long haul. Her hand shook a bit as the nicotine hit her system.

Ryan said he was there about her son, Ricky Cutts.

She nodded. "Yup. He was here last night," she said. She let out a long stream of smoke down the conference table.

Oh. "He was?" Ryan asked. "What did he say?"

She looked at him with visible contempt. "Don't be a dumbass. How could he say anything? He's dead. Murdered. Dead and done, one by one. He just wandered around my room half the night, all wet and dripping, don't go slipping."

"How did you hear he was dead?" Ryan asked.

"Cigarette," she said again. The attendant left and returned with a second one. She tucked it away. Ryan waited. She finally answered the question hanging in the air, saying, trying to be casual, "Heard it around." Her hand jerked.

Ryan asked what she thought about what had happened to Ricky.

"Cigarette," she said. Ryan realized that she was meeting with him only to obtain the smokes, which probably had been taken away as a privilege for some kind of failure to cooperate. He asked the assistant superintendent if they could speed things up by giving her an entire pack.

Mrs. Cutts, listening to this, smiled. She had won. "Well, I know who killed him," she said softly, as if to reward him for deducing her little ruse.

Ryan waited. She lit another cigarette off the butt of the first. She puffed on the new one. "You people," she said, lifting her chin. "You ignore me, you laugh at me, you put me away in this jail, like it's all my fault. Then, when you want something, then you act nice. But you are not, you're like snot."

Ryan waited.

She leaned forward. "Okay, I'll tell you," she said. "Who killed Ricky? Who killed my son?" Then she snarled, "*Men!* They kill everything. Ring a ding ding." She jabbed her cigarette downward but leaned just beyond the ashtray and instead ground the burning butt into the back of Ryan's hand. "Pain," she snarled, as if introducing him to the subject. Ryan looked at his hand in surprise, then brushed off the ember. She spat into his face. The standing attendant, leaping forward, put his hands on her shoulders. She looked directly at Ryan for the first time. "Get the fuck out of here!" she shouted.

The assistant superintendent silently pointed Ryan toward the men's room across the lobby, as if this meeting had gone exactly as she had expected. When Ryan emerged from the washroom, he saw Shirley Cutts being led down the hallway at the back of the lobby, an attendant on either side. "FBI, spit in your eye!" she was shouting in a singsong voice. "Cock-a-doodle-doo, asshole!"

Nothing like family, he thought to himself. *All in a day's work.* He sat in his truck and tried to think through the meeting. The only point of substance was her observation that men kill everything. In terms of crime statistics, she was more or less correct, he thought. But it didn't tell him much that he could see.

He pushed the truck's start/stop button and put his hands on the wheel. But as he did, a wave of physical emotion hit him. He pushed the button again to turn off the engine, sat back and wept. *That poor, wretched wreck of an old woman*, he thought. He hated to think of what it must be like to be trapped inside her head. She had been shattered by life. And so had he. He cried for them both for several minutes.

VISITING ROCKFISH

Then, for the first time, he drove down the west side of Penobscot Bay, the opposite side of the bay from Liberty Island. He kept the window open to have a breeze across his face, still hot from the session with Mrs. Cutts.

Belfast, with its business center of brick stores on a hillside descending toward a harbor crowded with red-and-black tugboats, felt like a "normal" Maine town to him, like Liberty or Ellsworth. He had been told that Belfast had gentrified a bit and wasn't as rough as it had felt back in the mid-twentieth century when the major waterfront business had been a chicken processing plant that tossed the birds' guts into the bay, a practice that attracted great white sharks looking for a fast meal. They swam up the bay, just under the surface, looming like some kind of submarine Greyhound bus. The sight of their triangular, gray forward dorsal fins slicing through the harbor, along with the rich and complex odors from gassy bubbles emanating from chicken parts rotting in the bottom mud, had tended to deter tourists. The attractiveness of the town began to improve after the poultry processing plan closed down in 1988. The jobs were missed, but not working in "the blood tunnel," as the plant's workers called the hardest part of the factory, where panicked chickens who had evaded the automatic execution machines were finished off.

South of Belfast, the changes in the scenery surprised him. The houses along Route 1 took on a moneyed sheen, especially in Camden. Everything was trimmer, fresher, newly painted, a bit too well kept to feel like the real Maine he was coming to know. There were no rusting car parts or boat winches piled in front yards. It was like the college town of Cambridge, Massachusetts, had decided to establish a colony in Maine—and that was indeed pretty much what happened. There were no potholes here to rattle the shiny new high-end hybrid SUVs that packed its downtown.

He followed the coastal highway through Camden to Rockfish and turned right to the medical examiner's office. It was at the small hospital, conveniently adjacent to the emergency room. A cheerful, short woman with spiky black hair and who walked with roll, as if she were a sailor just ashore after a transocean voyage, came across the room to greet him.

He saw by her plastic name tag that she was Dr. Peyton. She looked him up and down, seemingly surprised by his appearance. "Didn't think you'd be so young," she said. "I guess I assumed you'd be older, like your predecessor." Ryan sighed inwardly. They all expected the FBI man from Bangor to be a broken-down work-horse put out to pasture.

He followed her into the tiny two-table morgue. His knees weakened but did not buckle. She glanced at his face and said, "You okay?"

"Yes," he said. But he knew she could tell he wasn't. He looked woozy. He felt like little bubbles of gas were floating up through his brain. "Actually, I feel a bit lightheaded," he confessed.

She had seen people react to the morgue this way before. She knew it couldn't be the first time an FBI agent had been in one, so she calculated that his ashen face was caused by personal reasons, probably family history. She always said that you can't really know a person, or a corpse, without knowing the family they came from. "Sit down here," she said, pulling up a brown folding metal chair. She went to the water cooler and returned with a paper cup. "Sip this," she advised. "Take your time."

They chatted about Maine for a while as he collected himself. He had come from California, he said. She replied that she was from "the County, about a six-hour drive north of here."

He seemed grateful for the diversion and asked what she remembered from her childhood there. "Potatoes," she began. "The sun going down at three in the afternoon in December. Logging trucks rumbling slowly on the roads, dropping chunks of bark and dirt when they hit a bump. Being lesbian and lonely in high school. I really don't miss much about it except for the *ployes*." Those, she explained, are buckwheat pancakes served piping hot with butter for breakfast, or as a side bread with a brothy evening stew. And, she said, "Solid has learned to cook a pretty good version of those."

When the color came back into his face, they arose and moved next to the body on the table. Work had been quiet, she explained, so she not only examined the head wound but also checked out the entire state of the corpse. "This guy's body was fifteen years older than it should have been."

"Lots of wear and tear from fishing?"

"That and more." Incipient heart disease, with bad arteries. Bad knees, an eroded meniscus in each. Knuckles gnarled with arthritis, "probably from constant repeated immersion in cold seawater." Liver bloated. Lungs? She pointed with the scalpel to brown tar smears on them, signs of years of smoking. But there had been almost no water in them, "which means he had stopped breathing before he was placed in the sea."

"What do you make of the head wound?" Ryan asked.

"Pretty simple," she said. "There were two blows; either one could have been lethal. As you've seen, the second one lay slightly crosswise and behind the first, less on the top of the skull and a bit more to the back."

"So he was facing his attacker when he was first hit?" Ryan asked.

"Can't tell. Could have been from behind—depends on the angle of approach."

"And the second blow?

"Don't like to guess, but that angle of the impact indicates it probably was delivered after Cutts was down."

"What can you tell about the assault weapon?"

"Something long, metal, heavy. And a bit uneven in shape." She pointed to a spot in the skull where the wound was wider. "Not just a piece of pipe or rebar, for example. Some kind of tool, maybe. But not a hammer, which leaves a very different pattern, more concentrated and deeper, which usually lacerates the scalp. Maybe a wrench. Heavy enough to crush, broad enough not to cut much."

He looked impressed. "Any other thoughts?"

"This was not a happy man," she said.

Ryan looked intrigued. "How does an autopsy tell you that?"

"A basic rule is to consider who shows up to collect the body. Gives me context."

"And?" Ryan said.

"No one has. Not even a phone call. Tells me he's either lonely or unwanted." She asked if Cutts had any living relatives.

"Yes," Ryan said, "two daughters, apparently alienated from him. An elderly mother, hospitalized and incompetent. And a dead wife in Baltimore."

Dr. Peyton shook her head. "Another catastrophic family," she said softly. She was entirely unsurprised. Her work had taught her over the years that tragedy comes in bunches because despair is infectious, transmitted through harsh words, angry blows, substance abuse, and premature deaths.

Ryan's phone rang. It was Harriet. He indicated to the examiner that he needed to take it.

He walked to a corner. As was Harriet's habit, she immediately told him what was on her mind. "The Malpense have filed a complaint against you," she said without a greeting. She was not happy. "Ryan! I thought I told you not to fuck with the Indians!"

He was staggered. "About what?" He realized he had never heard Harriet curse before.

The tribal council's official complaint to the State Police stated that the FBI man had pulled over a driver in Calais who turned out to be a member of the northern Malpense. "They said you'd been abusive, hauled the driver out of his car, pushed him against the side of his car. Hard. And they say they have photos." She paused. "Ryan, what the hell is going on? You know I told you about being careful."

"Harriet, this is a simple one," Ryan said. "I've never been to Calais. Or even near it. Ever."

She stopped and thought. "Okay," she said. "But this is still delicate. Until the allegation is sorted out, your investigation is suspended. All your investigations. You are off duty."

"I hear you, Harriet."

"You better." She hung up.

Dr. Peyton looked at him with concern. "Bad news?"

"Yeah," he said. His face was ashen again. In truth, he could barely hear her over the buzzing in his head. "I, uh, have to stop asking you questions."

She examined his face. "You need to lie down and rest," she said. She said she'd let Solid know that his visit over there would be postponed. She shook her head. "You are carrying some kind of load, I can tell that."

"Not here," he said, emphatically shaking his head. The idea of lying down in a morgue made his stomach turn over.

"Well, you can't drive in your condition," she said. Her sharp tone indicated that she wasn't just suggesting—she was speaking as a medical professional.

"I'll just walk across the parking lot and sit in my truck until I feel better," he said.

"You need to rest for at least half an hour," she replied. "Eyes closed, no phone calls."

She handed him another cup of water. He sat in the truck for a full hour. When that was up, he decided to take another fifteen minutes. He was reeling mentally. He sipped from the cup, closed his eyes, tried not to think. But the Malpense complaint kept rolling around in his mind. What sort of message was being sent?

When his head felt clearer, he pulled out and began the drive home. He drove slowly, carefully. Yet after about twenty miles, when he was just entering Belfast, a huge wave of fatigue rolled over him. He pulled into the corner of the parking lot at an Aubuchon Hardware store and dozed for fifteen minutes. He awoke with a start, momentarily unsure of where he was. When he was oriented, he resumed the drive to his cottage. *I'm back on the Tilt-A-Whirl*, he thought. His mind was a buzzing blank for most of the drive. *Home?* he thought hazily as he got out of his truck.

In the bathroom he saw his face in the mirror and barely recognized it. His eyes seemed to be contorted with agony. Again he felt faint, almost like there were black shutters pushing in on the outside of his eyes. He pulled an Ensolite pad out of the bedroom closet and gathered up the big blue sleeping bag he used as a bed-cover. He carried them to the back porch and wrapped the bag around himself. He lay down on the pad. The world looked black-and-white to him, all color drained. His life was collapsing. Family gone, with that rock-hard reminder in the morgue today. A cluster of lawsuits back in San Diego that nagged at him but offered no peace. Living a solitary existence. Shirley Cutts putting out her cigarette in his hand and then spitting in his face. He looked down at the little red blister on the back of his hand. And now, the last thing that kept him going—his work—taken from him. He felt adrift. Close to unhinged. Was he following Mrs. Cutts down the pathway of madness? Even with the sleeping bag around him, he shivered. He had been walking on thin ice. Now he was crashing through it.

He awoke once to the stars. Lying on his back, looking up at the sky, he could see, among the stars, an occasional satellite slowly swimming across the heavens—moving faster than the stars but slower than the transatlantic jets, with their blinking green and red lights at the ends of their wings. He heard the high, soft chuckle of a loon. He listened to the light wind brush the pines and then went back to sleep.

How long he slept, he did not know. It was light. Then was it dark again? He didn't really care. His sleep was dreamless as far as he could tell. He didn't care if he ever moved again.

A NUDGE

Then it was light once more. He was awakened by something nudging him. With his eyes closed, he half-dreamed that an animal had wandered up onto the porch. He opened his eyes and saw Harriet standing over him, pushing the toe of her sneaker into his shoulder. From his supine position she looked enormously tall, like a talking statue. Her head seemed to be somewhere quite remote, up in the clouds. Her hands were on her hips.

She told him—really ordered him—to wake up. "Tapia!" she said loudly. She leaned over and sniffed him. Her field outfit was a cognate of his—hers was a white oxford shirt, Lands' End khakis, and black sneakers that looked more like shoes. Over the shirt she wore a black blazer, a size too large, the better to accommodate her shoulder holster, which was black nylon. This was the FBI's idea of style.

He eased himself out of the sleeping bag, slowly stood, and went inside. There he brushed his teeth, took a shower, shaved, dressed in fresh clothes, made two cups of coffee, and took them out to the back porch, where she was sitting in a deck chair and gazing at her smartphone. She accepted the coffee wordlessly and put away her phone. There was a cool briskness in her he hadn't seen before. A distance. She was in decision-making mode.

"Look, Ryan. I emailed you, I texted, and I called. When I didn't hear back, I got in my truck this morning and drove up. When I got here, I knocked and knocked. Front door was locked. I called again. No answer.

"So I walked around the cottage to find you here, splayed out on the back deck, like you were sleeping one off. How long have you been out?"

"I don't know," he confessed. "After you called me about the Malpense complaint, I drove here, and I just felt comatose, like the deepest sugar low ever."

"I worried you were drunk or something," she said. He realized that was why she had leaned in and sniffed.

"I'm not—just worn out," he reassured her.

"Good, because I actually have good news for you. You're cleared of the Malpense complaint. The man in the photographs, the one who claimed to be an FBI agent? He was shorter, older, and heavier than you. The State Police have identified him by make and color of his vehicle. They've arrested him on felony imperson-ation charges. His vehicle has red-and-blue flashers in his grill. Clearly some kind of police wannabe. The Staties said they've notified the Malpense Council that you and the bureau have been absolved of any wrongdoing in the matter."

Ryan noticed that she had made sure that the bureau was cleared too. "You did all that in just a few hours, since we talked?" Ryan asked. He was impressed. He saluted her with his coffee cup.

Harriet looked at him sharply. "I talked to you on Tuesday afternoon," she said. "This is Thursday morning. Jesus, you must have been conked out here for, what, a night, a day, another night—that's, like, thirty-six hours." Her forehead furrowed. "Ryan, when did you last eat? And what was it?"

"I don't know," he confessed.

She shook her head, slowly. Message: *Not good enough, Agent Tapia.*

"I feel better now," he protested. "Ready to go back to work."

She shook her head again. "Not gonna happen," she said. "This is what you are going to do, in order.

"First, you get a decent meal or two in you. Second, you get a medical examination. Third, you have the doctor call me, directly. Until then, no Agent Tapia on duty. Got it?"

She wrote down the name and number of a Dr. Healey in Bangor. "I've worked with him in the past."

She stood. "Again, until I hear from him, you're benched," she emphasized, pointing a finger at him. "I need to have confidence in you. You have not been practicing self-care. So consider yourself on a kind of informal probation, nothing official, just between you and me. No official record.

"One last thing," she said, looking down at him. "I want a drug test. Comprehensive. Screening for everything from meth to opioids."

His eyes widened. "You think I'm on something?" he asked.

"No, I don't," she said, "but a good manager makes sure." To herself, she thought: Tapia, maybe you *should* be on something. And I've worked too hard to get my current position to screw it up by going too easy on you. She also thought that if Ryan didn't start eating right, he might really need to be suspended. He looked emaciated, and that meant his physical and mental reserves would be limited. You never knew in this job when you'd need to go to surge capacity and work twenty-four hours straight.

He knew she was right. "Thank you," he said slowly. He worried that he sounded grudging, so he added, "I mean it." Given his state, she needed to cover herself. Any self-respecting FBI manager would do the same. As soon as she left, he got on it. First, he microwaved and ate a frozen Salisbury steak dinner that had been in the freezer for months. Then he called the doctor's scheduler, who jumped at the "special request from the FBI." She said Dr. Healey had been planning on taking the day off to go trout fishing but might be willing to stop by his office to see Ryan on his way. A minute later she called back to confirm the plan. "He'll be here soon," she said.

Ryan hurried out to his truck. There he saw a second note on the dashboard, taped below the first one, which was his self-reminder to ask follow-up questions. He recognized Harriet's handwriting, torn from her work notebook. The new note said, "And eat right." He sat for a minute and contemplated that, then went back into the house and found an apple in the refrigerator. Back in the truck, a few miles passed before the second thought passed through his head: Harriet had gone snooping through his truck—and with that note was telling him so. What else was he being slow to apprehend?

Dr. Ed Healey was dressed for his fishing excursion in khakis, a long-sleeved plaid shirt, and a down vest. He was a big man, with the hulking but intelligent look of a defensive lineman, which in fact had been his position on the undefeated Dartmouth football team, the Ivy League champions of 1996. He had not been a fast runner, but he was smart and nimble. He could read a play and react quickly. And he had heft. Like many of Maine's doctors, Healey was an outdoorsman who had been lured to the state by the quick access to hunting and fishing spots. He drew a vial of blood from Ryan and sent it down the hall to the lab with "ASAP" scrawled on the white label.

Ryan gave him a summary of his life over the last year, beginning with the accident. Healey expressed his sympathy and began the examination, making notes and saying little. "Breathe deeply. . . . Left eye open wide. . . . Right one now. . . . Run on this machine, and keep going as the ramp elevates. . . . Good, seeing the heart rate." A whack with a triangular rubber hammer on one knee, then the other.

An assistant walked in and handed the doctor several sheets of paper. "Printout from the blood lab," Healey said and sat down behind his desk. He read it slowly, a pen in hand, making check marks and notes. He took a surprisingly long time, flipping back and forth, checking numbers against each other. Ryan began to feel as if he were on trial.

Healey looked up and said, "Agent Tapia, I want to thank you for coming in today. This is one of the more interesting profiles I've ever seen." He dictated into his laptop: "Male, Caucasian, thirty-two years old, federal law enforcement officer. Height, six one; weight, 132. We will speak about that." He looked up at Ryan to make sure he heard, then returned to his narration to the laptop. "Severe family trauma within previous twelve months. Presents as normal psychologically. Two troublesome signs: Cholesterol is through the roof, like he's living on eggs." At this, Ryan nodded woefully. "Potassium is low." He paused. "No indication of drug abuse."

He swiveled from the computer to Ryan. He said he would call Harriet and give her that green light. Ryan began to thank him, but Healey held up his hand, giving the flat "stop" sign.

"On three conditions," he said. First, he said, Ryan needed to clean up his diet. "Vary it, eat lots of dark vegetables like spinach and broccoli, every night, and a banana or two every morning. Eggs just once a week." He paused and looked over Ryan. "You know, I'm a healthy specimen, and I weigh nearly twice what you do." He also prescribed over-the-counter potassium pills for the next several months.

Ryan nodded.

Second, he insisted that Ryan see a grief counselor. He wrote down the name of a woman down in Hallowell who specialized in working with law enforcement officers—both those who had suffered from violence and those who had inflicted it. "She gets a lot of work," Dr. Healey said as he handed the paper to him. "Being a game warden in this state can be tough duty. Most of the people they deal with are armed, and many of them are drunk. It's a dangerous mix."

Ryan took the slip and nodded again. "Third?" Ryan asked.

"You need to relax a bit. Maybe try some marijuana in the evening, if your job rules permit that. And I want you, right now, to take off the next two days." Ryan said he would, as much as possible, but that he had a couple of people he had to see.

The doctor stood before Ryan did. "If anyone needs me," he shouted toward the front desk, "I'll be at Caratunk Falls on the Kennebec." He strode out the door, still a quick man on his feet.

Ryan followed. He left the doctor's office feeling reenergized. Back in his truck, he called Solid Harrison. She said it was indeed a good time to come on down, because her morning rush was nearly over, so Ryan pulled out of the parking lot and headed south. He stopped and bought a bunch of bananas and ate them as he drove.

THE HIGH-END MARKET

In Rockfish, Solid Harrison's Top Shelf Fish market stood out on the working waterfront. It was painted bright white, with cheerful flower boxes brimming with geraniums and violets hanging under the two windows. The front of the building held a small, spare, tidy business office. The back part of the building, where Harrison kept her inventory and prepared it for shipment, was built on pilings out over the harbor, with a dock below where her suppliers could tie up their boats and make their deliveries to her.

Solid met him at the door. "Feeling better?" she asked. He nodded. She was slightly taller than him, perhaps two inches above six feet. Everything about her was long—her arms, her legs, her neck. "We can talk while I work," she told him, leading him to the back. An opera was playing.

"The fish like this music?" Ryan said.

"*The Magic Flute*," Solid said. "I do." She told Alexa to pause. Even in her black fishing boots, she had an air of elegance to her, with lively green eyes, a wise smile, and long brown hair with strands of gray beginning to show, tied and held in place on her back by a blue-and-green silk scarf. Many women of her height might dress in a way that de-emphasized that characteristic, but she embraced it. She was wearing blue-and-white-striped pants that made her legs seem impossibly extended. She had a large forehead that Ryan found attractive, like a sign saying that there was a lot going on behind it.

She said they could talk while she did some routine tasks in the holding room such as checking oxygen levels and water temperatures, keeping an eye on the state of her inventory and thinking about tomorrow's buying needs, and generally making sure that nothing went out that was not the absolute best.

"The high-end fish trade? Well, on this part of the coast, that's pretty much me." She didn't say it with pride, just with a sober assessment. It was a niche business.

"How did you get into it?"

"I was a rebel, but against hippie-ism. My parents were potheads. Still are. Good people, but their total lack of rules made me crave regulation and order, seek it out wherever possible. You know how to make sure your daughter graduates from high school a virgin? Tell her that her boyfriends are welcome to sleep over.

"The result of that raising was that all my life, I was good at seeing the structure, of what you need to do in a given place to thrive. First in my class at high school. Full scholarship to Orono."

"What's Orono?"

She looked at him. "Wow, you really are fresh off the boat," she said, but not in an unfriendly way. "That's the main campus of the University of Maine. 'Go Black Bears.' I did well there, first in class again. Then Harvard Law, where I got interested in aviation law, mainly commercial litigation, with a lot of fights over leasing issues.

"I wound up joining a Boston firm. Partner track at twenty-eight, bored at thirty-five, burning out by thirty-eight. I was up here in early June a few years ago, visiting my parents, when a neighbor came over with a big chunk of halibut. People do that here, sharing their bounty. And he probably remembered it was my favorite fish. We grilled it that evening out back over an oak fire. Just marvelous with a light sesame and ginger sauce.

"That night, I was falling asleep, staring out the window at the blanket of stars that I couldn't ever see from my house in Brookline. And I wondered, why can't I get fish like that anywhere else? I should be able to.

"I woke up the next morning and began to plan a new business." On a yellow pad, she had listed three key factors: "With the growth of FedEx and other delivery systems, I could ship anywhere in the country in a chiller and have it there the next day. Literally, a lobster or fish could be hauled out one morning in Maine and served in a restaurant in Kansas City the next evening. Then there was a new generation of chefs coming up, more interested in top quality, and with patrons who would pay for it. It's a micromarket, one or maybe two restaurants at most in, say, a place like Nashville or Pittsburgh."

The calculations on the pad mounted. "I figured I could break even with fifteen client restaurants getting my weekly shipments, and probably make good money with twenty or so. That meant the business could stay small. I didn't want to become a manager.

"A year later, I was in business. Started fast, got faster. I topped out at about six shipments a day, forty a week," she said.

"And the third key factor?" Ryan asked. He found this account somehow fascinating—perhaps as much because of who was speaking as her subject.

"Familiarity," she said. "I grew up here. I knew a lot of the people who fish here, went to high school with them. That's important. Takes time to build trust. They knew my face, and that counts for a lot around here." She didn't say it, but she knew that, to many of them, she was still that, "tall smart girl" who had been pretty good at basketball and also was class president and valedictorian.

Nor did Solid mention to Ryan that she had learned about the distribution business from her father, who was one of the major marijuana growers on the coast, with a big greenhouse on a remote, southward-facing hillside in a vale in the woods west of Belfast. While in high school she had helped him keep his books. One of the lessons she had learned then was that the cost, reliability, and availability of labor can sneak up on you, especially if they are helping themselves to the wares.

"The high-end fish business took off, too fast, really," she said. The demand surprised her. After some early hiccups, she had capped her client list at thirty restaurants around the country. "Each gets a weekly shipment—lobster, oysters, scallops, whatever good fish is running, and maybe specialty items like sea urchins. And every winter I take a month to drive around the country, eating at each client's place. Most of them are really good, so it's a pleasure. But I've dropped a few who really didn't know how to appreciate a good fish. I mean, don't bread and deep-fry my fish and ask me to be happy."

"You can fire customers?" Ryan had never heard of such a thing.

"Sure can. Treat my fish right and pay your bills on time, or take a hike. I keep a waiting list." She didn't say it, but chefs sometimes mentioned her business by name in listing their specials. In the trade it was called "menu boasting."

"What about the other specialty market?"

Solid cocked an eyebrow, lowered her chin, and looked over her eyeglasses. "You mean sturgeon, big wolffish, oversize tuna, exotic sharks, and such." It wasn't a question.

"Yes," he said.

"Because I've never heard of the FBI being into fish before," she said.

"Not the fish itself," he said. "That's a job for NOAA's fisheries office. But because of a possible tie to the death of Ricky Cutts."

She dove right in, talking more quickly. "That backdoor market, that's the exact opposite of my business. My model is a steady flow of shipments to known customers, who each buy from me about forty times a year. I give them dependable quality, and they give me regular orders that keeps the cash flow healthy. Fast, fresh, frequent, and federally compliant—that's my mantra."

She reached down to turn over an oyster, examined it, frowned slightly, and then threw it out an open window. Ryan heard a small splash when it hit the harbor water.

"But sturgeon and shark, and even tuna," she said. "That business is one-off big spenders, usually executive chefs working on Wall Street or big law firms. Private equity firm that wants to impress visiting Japanese businessmen? Slap a ten-foot Atlantic sturgeon on the table. Not only great fish, but one that officially doesn't exist anymore around here. What could be more exotic? There are people who love that sort of nonsense.

"I've been offered absolutely obscene amounts of cash for big fresh bluefin tuna in midwinter, when there are few around and the seas are freezing and rough." The money was as much to compensate for the danger and discomfort as for the rarity of the fish.

"They go for sharks too?"

"Yeah, mainly litigators and people who want to show how tough they are when the fixers and European bankers for Russian oligarchs drop by. Celebrate a legal victory by rolling a shortfin mako into the conference room. What pisses me off is I hear they sometimes don't even eat it." She turned to make a few notations and check marks about temperature and oxygen levels on a white-board. "That's disrespectful of the fish and of nature."

"You ever meet Ricky Cutts?"

She stopped working and walked to the eastern end of the room, to the big picture window overlooking the docks. She had a hose running from a float four hundred feet out, pumping the cold clean water of the bay through her tanks. From the window, she could see which boats were heading in and who would be tying up. She could consider then what she might say to them, and what price adjustments might be needed. "Just once," she replied. "Early in the Covid time, Ricky Cutts came in saying he had a prime bluefin for me. I knew just looking at him I probably wasn't going to buy, so I told him I wasn't in the market for tuna that week, but that I'd like to see the fish anyway." She figured that he had come to her because his regular buyers had been knocked off track by the pandemic, with a lot of chefs being thrown off stride by virus-related restrictions.

"Why would his appearance put you off buying his tuna?"

She shook her head slightly. "I mean, I'm no snob—the boys come in here reeking of fish and sea muck from here to next week. But this guy just looked unhealthy, runny nose, red eyes, some kind of rash on the side of his neck. That all tells me, that is not a guy focused on quality issues. And my business is all about that. No cut corners, no cheap compromises." It was clear that to her Ricky Cutts embodied the opposite of those standards.

"So when we got down to his boat, its appearance confirmed my reluctance. Rusty cleats, hull needed paint, rope tangled in a corner with a dead crab. Slovenly. It smelled. Not the healthy odors of seaweed and sea air, but a kind of rot."

"What was the tuna like?"

"Lying on the deck near the stern. He'd dumped ice over it, but it looked like it might have some engine oil on it. I don't know how the hell that happened."

"So you wouldn't buy it?"

"I had no choice. It was maybe nine feet long, and that's too big to be legal. So I thanked him and sent him on his way. He shrugged and left, like he had expected to be disappointed. But there was a kind of pent-up look in his face, like at his next stop he'd describe me as 'that stuck-up bitch.' I don't need that attitude on my dock."

"Where do you think his regular buyer was?" Ryan asked.

She knew the likely answer: This guy from New York comes in a refrigerated truck, not every week. Usually shows up on Wednesdays. Picks up a load at about sunset, runs it down to New York overnight. Pays top dollar, always cash. But instead, she said to Ryan, "Tell you what. You visit a few other seafood dealers, the big lobster wholesalers, down in Rockland and over in Friendship. Give me some cover. Then, if you still need to, come back to me maybe in a week or so."

That sounded reasonable to Ryan.

They walked out into the small parking lot. As they stood together, she offered one more thought. "I have to tell you," she began, "I don't really see anyone killing this guy over fish. People do get angry. But it's a business, and murder is bad for business. No offense, but it brings visits from people like you.

"Someone has a problem, there are ample punitive steps short of homicide. A buyer could cut off a seller. He or she could spread the word to other buyers, and blackball the seller from the trade. I heard of one middleman who kind of accidentally, but maybe not, let a rope slip while lowering a hundred-pound basket of fermented bait ten feet to a boat deck. It went splattering all over the boat.

"If you wanted to be subtle, you could turn off the automatic bilge pump in a guy's boat just before a big storm. It would then take on water, and, sinking lower, when the storm hit, would let waves come over the side. And if you really wanted to make an unmistakable statement, you could torch a boat. But that's kind of like going to war. Most people are too smart for that."

She looked squarely at him. "I know this waterfront pretty well—I mean the working side of it, not the yacht side," she said. "People talk. Maybe I flatter myself, but I think if someone had a real beef with Ricky Cutts over a fishing issue, something getting out of hand, I would have heard something. I haven't."

He thanked her and thought about her words of wisdom on the drive back to Bangor. This time, the Hank Williams lyric that caught his ear was, "Hear that lonesome whippoorwill. He sounds too blue to fly." It occurred to him that Solid Harrison was someone who had built a new life starting in her thirties. He admired that. Maybe it was not too late for him, he hoped. He didn't quite admit it to himself, but he found her slender coolness alluring. She had an intensity to her, a piercing intelligence, that caught his attention. Her dark green eyes had looked straight into his. She was what, in times past, was called "a tall drink of water." Many people as tall as her were ungainly. She was not. She was smooth and slender. And she exuded intelligence and self-confidence. She knew what she was about.

Back home, he called Harriet in Portland. He had taken her hint and was reporting in every day, not waiting for her to check on him. He said he was learning a lot. "Did you know that by treaty, the Indian tribes of Maine hold three seats in the state legislature?" he said. "It's the only state that has that." He hoped his demonstration of sensitivity to tribal issues was noticed.

"Ah, you're starting to get Maine," she said, clearly pleased. She offered him another detail on that issue: the tribal members of the legislature don't have votes, and they don't feel they are listened to by state lawmakers, so the tribal leaders have redesignated their own members of the legislatures as "ambassadors." "Like to a foreign nation," she added.

He told her that the fishing trade angle wasn't leading anywhere. "So it's back to the drug business?" she asked. Yes, he said. It was time to visit Abby Buck again.

Harriet had one other item to review. "By the way, did you, uh, know there's word going around that you met with a CIA recruiter the other day?"

So pompous old Bissell was still stirring the shit, making trouble for him, Ryan thought. *What other phone calls had that guy been making?* he wondered. "I wouldn't call it a job interview," he told his boss. "Guy was doing his best to piss me off. Is that how they recruit?" He explained the circumstances of his meeting with the professorial CIA officer.

Harriet laughed. She was satisfied with his account—and actually had more to add to it. "Typical CIA bullshit," she said. "Ever since 9/11, we've been butting heads with them over operations in the Middle East." She didn't say it, but the feuding between the agency and the bureau went back decades earlier, to when Director Hoover had made a bid to control all American espionage operations around the world. President Truman didn't trust Hoover and instead had created the CIA. Since then, their cultures had clashed constantly. The FBI saw itself as peopled by lower middle-class strivers, while viewing the agency as loaded with moneyed dilletantes. The bureau recruited from state universities, while the agency still favored Ivy League graduates. No less an authority than Harold "Kim" Philby, the most notorious British traitor of the twentieth century, once commented that FBI men were "proud of their insularity, of having sprung from the grass roots." For its part, the CIA saw the FBI as shortsighted and all too eager to publicize its operations, which it saw as unseemly in an intelligence organization. Agency officers contended that by contrast, their successes were always kept under wraps.

As for Bissell's account, Harriet told Ryan that about seven or so of the retired CIA station chiefs living in Maine met for lunch once a month in Camden. She had heard through the federal grapevine that Bissell had attended the sit-down just the other day and had regaled the table with his tale of how he had intimidated this clumsy FBI man nosing around Liberty Island.

"Sounds to me like the story has grown with the retelling," Ryan said grumpily.

Then, keeping his promise to Dr. Healey, Ryan sat on the back deck, sipped a few IPAs, and read more of this strange book Wundermin had sent about what kind of people the author saw survive concentration camps.

BACK TO BUCK

The next morning Ryan called ahead to Abby Buck, then drove down to Liberty. The drug dealer walked out to Ryan's truck. Something was on his mind. "Agent Tapia, I suspect you're here because you've ruled out the fishing business as a cause of Ricky Cutts's demise."

That's right, said Ryan, even now surprised that Abby Buck seemed so well informed about his movements and conversations. He got out of his truck. Buck had not mentioned to him that one of his major marijuana suppliers was Solid Harrison's father. Over the years, "Natural" Harrison's dope, with its dark green, almost black leaves, brimming with bristling, tarry buds, had acquired a sterling reputation as the top shelf THC in the region. Mr. Harrison was dedicated to his business, keeping a string of horses and donkeys mainly for their manure, which the marijuana plants loved. Buck reserved Harrison's stuff for his favored customers. Ryan knew nothing of all that.

"But you still think it could be the drug business that did him in, somehow?" Buck said. He appeared genuinely curious about Ryan's thinking.

"Well, what else could it be?" Ryan said. The two of them leaned on the corners at the back of the truck's bed, as men in Maine often do when they are having a serious, "no shit" discussion.

Buck stared at Ryan for a minute. Ryan could not discern what he was thinking. Finally, Buck said, "Did I tell you about my foray into the pizza business?"

"No," Ryan said, wondering where this was going.

Buck scanned the tree line out of habit. "Last winter," he began, "I was bored, restless. Hovering over my employees too much."

"Like how?" Ryan asked. He was genuinely interested that a drug dealer devoted so much care to how he managed subordinates. But it made sense, he considered—nothing could send an illegal business south faster than a disgruntled employee.

"One thing I've learned is, you've got to step back and let people make mistakes. That's how they learn. But I was visiting each store manager every day, asking what they were gonna do about this clerk not showing up for a shift on time, second-guessing how they handled it.

"For me, I've learned that boredom is a sign that it's time for me to open a new line of business. So I began researching delivering pizzas. It's an interesting business problem. There's good steady money in it, but no one has been able to make it work on this part of the coast because the population is scattered in little towns at the end of a series of long peninsulas. And half the year, the potholes and fog and snow make driving slow and even hazardous. In a nutshell, if it takes thirty minutes to deliver a pizza and as much time again to get back to the store, there's no way to pay a decent wage and also make a profit. You'd have to charge fifty bucks a pie.

"So," Buck said, "I thought, how about using drones to deliver pizza?" From Liberty Island to Rockfish, he explained, took ninety minutes by land, but was only ten miles as the crow flies straight across the bay. "I ran the numbers—four people working nine hours a day, five days a week, making and flying out about a hundred pizzas a day. One person to take orders, two to make the pies, and the fourth to operate four drones, punching in delivery addresses and monitoring their flights."

He spent months on the project. "Bought ten different drones and started flying test routes carrying pizzas from the three Downeast Depots." Some of the aircraft, he found, simply were too underpowered to maintain a reasonable speed against winter winds. Also, battery duration and strength turned out to be more of an issue than he had expected. "Someone across the bay orders the meat lover's special, weighed down with sausage, pepperoni, and meatballs, maybe extra cheese, onions, and green peppers, carrying all that into a headwind would slow down the delivery a lot," he had discovered. Still, Abby figured, after construction, labor, supplies, marketing, and insurance, he could make a bit of money on the flying pizza business, with small but dependable profit margins. "But I also would have given myself the headache of operating the busiest landing zone in Down East Maine. And I'd have a higher profile. Not good in my business."

"Then why do it?" Ryan asked.

"Well, because I could deliver other things," Abby explained. "That's the real attraction. Marijuana is legal in Maine now. So someone on a Friday night might order a pizza, on which I make a few bucks, but also thirty dollars of marijuana, on which I make twenty dollars. And then there are 'off menu' items."

"Oxy, coke, meth?" Ryan asked.

"Things of that nature, perhaps. That could be the real profit driver," Buck said. "But that led to a new problem, and that's my point."

"Oh?" Ryan said, wondering where this was going.

Dealers in other towns got wind of what he was contemplating. "They realized that if my plan worked, I'd be the Jeff Bezos of Down East dope," he said, pronouncing the billionaire retailer's name correctly, as "bay-zos." It would not take long for him to drive them all out of business. So about five of his closest competitors had gotten together to drink a few beers and devise a response. They emerged with a private contest: shoot down as many of Buck's drones as you could. The person who got the most won $5,000. "They called it 'Get Lucky with Bucky.' They'd hide in the woods near my Depots where I was doing test runs. After six of my drones were shot down, I dropped the idea."

"Gave you pause, eh?" said Ryan.

"Yes," Buck said. "But it was the last one that really persuaded me. See, I'd expected maybe a couple of guys with shotguns. This is Maine, after all, and the guys are into fun and games." But, he continued, "Then one of them organized a laser ambush, blasted one of my drones with three different beams that fried out the electronics on my drone, and the poor thing just flew blindly out to sea.

"That last one took some work and research. They had to obtain lasers, figure out how to use them, organize the ambush on a route, and execute. And they did. That made me think carefully about where I am operating," he explained. "Bottom line is, you have to know where you are."

"And the moral of the story is?" Ryan said.

"You may find the island's ways odd, a throwback to a different time," Buck said. "But let me tell you this: most of the rest of the coast lost control of their places. Outsiders came in and took over the land, the politics, the schools. There's a town over on Mount Desert Island called Tremont. The locals running for selectmen put 'Tremont Native' on their roadside signs. It's kind of pathetic. If you have to say it, you've already lost control. Here on Liberty, we know who our natives are. No one needs to be told. And we run the island, not the from-aways."

"How did the locals here manage to escape the fate of other islands?" Ryan asked.

"Location, in part," Buck said. "We're well to the south of Route 1. Liberty is the only part of the Maine coast where it takes more than half an hour to drive to from that highway. That distance helps.

"But especially after the Depression, when a lot of people lost their land because of tax problems, the island learned to use legal means to defend itself. Every couple of years, you see a headline in the island's weekly newspaper, 'Selectmen Pass Growth Moratorium.' What that means is, some outsider has quietly bought a big parcel of land, usually being real quiet and sneaky about it, thinking that nobody sees them, and they've got notions of putting up hotels and condos and dense high-end housing, gonna make a bundle. But the selectmen keep an eye on that sort of secretive land transaction, someone from outside bundling on the sly, and when they get wind of it happening, they pass that rule that says no big developments for five years. Eventually the outsiders get the message that it ain't gonna happen. The carrying costs of the interest on the loan to buy the land make waiting five years too expensive. So they bail."

"And what should I take away from that?" Ryan said.

"Welcome to Maine, the real Maine," Buck said. "The point is recognizing where you are. You remember I told you that I've survived here because I understand the island, its ways. Life is different here. Real different. I mean, the way we live, the rules we live by. What we think of as common sense. Even if it makes no sense to off-islanders.

"Here's the point: You've got to consider the local point of view—and you can't assume it is the same as yours."

"Everyone keeps telling me that," he said. "What am I missing?"

"Okay, maybe you get it some," Buck said, "but maybe not enough." He looked at Ryan with what seemed to be genuine sympathy. "Look, you come from a world where only bad guys kill people, and they usually kill other bad guys. But that is not where you are now. Imagine another world, where good guys kill bad guys."

He looked around again, then back at Ryan. "You're the FBI man. But you don't understand. Look, everyone standing on this island today knows pretty much who killed Ricky Cutts. I mean, everyone except you. It's kind of sad. As a taxpayer, I expected more of the FBI." He turned from the truck and walked to the wooden stairs to his mobile home. "Ain't no mystery, Sherlock."

Ryan ignored the insult and looked up at him. "What did you mean by that?" he said.

Buck looked down at him, exasperated. His voice rose, and it wasn't just to compensate for the space between them. "You're turning over every rock on the island, seeing what crawls out," he said, throwing up an arm. "Dick Tracy detective work, gonna crack the case by finding a bad guy's fingerprints on a gun and such." He crouched a bit and mimed someone peering through a magnifying glass. "But what if the answer isn't under a rock? What if it is in plain sight? And what if the evidence is the opposite of what you are looking for?"

Ryan said nothing. He was taking it in, mulling what Buck was saying.

But Buck wasn't finished. "The funny thing is, Agent Tapia, people think that you, the FBI guy, know more than you do. Just the other day, you scared the shit out of our poor town manager."

"I did?" Ryan asked.

Buck smiled. "Freddy Ghent thinks you know why he really had to leave Gorland and take a little job up here. You show up in our little town, and he's getting all worried that you're maybe working on a public corruption case, you know."

"He didn't come here for that 'quieter pace of life' he told me about?" Ryan said.

"Well, that's what he tells people. But between us chickens, he has a little oxy problem," Buck said. "No biggie. What I hear is that he left his job in Gorland's town government after being offered a simple choice—immediate resignation with no severance pay, or face possible criminal charges."

Ryan considered that.

Buck added helpfully, "Freddy is keeping his usage low-level these days, by the way."

"And I guess you'd know that," Ryan said. "You give him a discount?"

"Don't know what you're talking about," Buck said with a smile that confirmed that he knew exactly what Ryan was talking about.

Ryan thanked him and got in his truck.

Buck stood on his front steps and watched the taillights of Ryan's truck head back down the driveway. He wondered if his talk had given the FBI man the nudge he needed. Buck would love to see Caleb Goodwin taken down a peg or two. But he would never confront Caleb directly. That would be madness. Buck was tolerated on the island, while Caleb was revered. Abby had wanted to push Ryan in the right direction without getting directly involved. He wondered if he had succeeded. He didn't know. He wished Agent Tapia was a little faster on the uptake. But then, unlike almost everyone else on the island, Buck knew what had happened to Ryan's family. Taking that devastation into account, he thought the FBI man was doing okay. Being a little slow sometimes was understandable.

ONE MORE CALL

Ryan drove back to Liberty's waterfront and parked. He thought through what Buck had said. He paged back through his case notes and came to his early encounter with Louise at Sarah's Shelter. She had encouraged Ryan to call her. He remembered a basic rule of investigating: Sometimes people will say on the phone what they won't say in person, for fear of being observed.

He dialed the number Louise had given him. "You said you might be able to help me," he began. "It's about Ricky Cutts."

Louise hemmed a bit. "You know I really can't talk about people."

But he sensed she had something she wanted to tell him. "One little thing—give me a hint," Ryan said. "What am I not seeing here?"

Louise's voice dropped to a whisper. "Without breaking confidentiality," she said, "I can tell you two women are here because of him, and a third should have been."

"Where's that third woman now?"

"Don't know. Heard she left the island. Maybe Portland. Or down Boston way."

"I'm going to need to talk to the Cutts girls," he said, knowing they were the "two women" she was referring to.

She refused. "That's not gonna happen." She explained, "Not out of a lack of willingness to help. But they have nothing to tell you." An edge of impatience crept into her voice. "Mister, it is time for you to get real. You've been barking up the wrong trees."

Ryan remembered that Abby Buck was the shelter's main financial backer. He wondered if Louise was covering for him somehow.

She put that notion to rest with her next words. "It wasn't drugs, or fish, that got Cutts killed," she said. "And the girls didn't do it. Think about it. It happened way down there on Ricky's fishing grounds. The girls don't have a boat. If someone gave them a ride down there, then word would get around. And they avoid their father as much as they can."

"But they might know who did it," Ryan said.

"They do not," Louise said. "I asked. But whoever it was, they are grateful."

"That's an interesting word to use, 'grateful.' Why?"

"I think I've said as much as I can," Louise said and hung up.

Well, that was a chunk of news. He got out of the truck to walk and think. He stood on the harbor's smaller dock, the one not reserved for fishermen, but rather the "yacht dock" where summertime sailboats and powerboats tied up. He gazed out at the archipelago to the southeast, looking in the direction of Ricky Cutts's distant fishing grounds. Then he strolled along the main street, past the tiny town library and the tourist shops. It was now June, and the place was filling up. He saw license plates from Rhode Island, Connecticut, New York, and especially Pennsylvania, Maryland, and Virginia. Why? He guessed that if you had to drive all the way to Maine from those mid-Atlantic states, why not add on a few hours and get to the less crowded, less expensive part of the coast, past Boothbay Harbor and Camden? Liberty Island was too far from Boston to make it a weekend escape from there, and that had kept down real estate prices.

The summer season had begun. He found his progress along the sidewalk slowed by tourists as it had not been a week earlier. He eavesdropped as he walked behind a couple wearing matching roll-necked tan cashmere sweaters. "It's all so cute," the woman was saying to the man, excitement in her voice. "I wish we could live here. It's like a fairy tale. The boats, the islands, the trees." They had all the time in the world to look at shop windows and gaze out across the harbor at the two windjammers moored there for the night, one with scarlet sails.

Ryan scoffed inwardly, thinking, *You chumps.* His talks with Abby Buck and with Louise at the shelter had left him in a sour mood. Trying to walk himself into a better state of mind, he moved along the length of the waterfront. He was thinking more than looking when he realized that Ghent, the town manager, was standing in front of him, almost frozen. The man's eyes were big in fear. He turned on his heel and began to walk away quickly.

"Mr. Ghent, wait!" Ryan shouted.

Ghent's pace increased. To his rattled ears, Ryan's urgency came across as, *Stop, in the name of the law.*

"Please!" Ryan added.

That seemed to work. Ghent stopped and turned. "What do you want?" he asked doubtfully, fear making his voice sound angry.

Ryan hesitated. He wanted to make a peace offering. "I want you to know—" he began, before he was cut off.

"To know what?" Ghent said. His oxycontin habit had kept him on thin ice for so long. Now, standing and looking at this FBI man, he felt like it was cracking underneath his feet. He had been run out of Gorland. He had finally landed here, at the end of the road, in a town well up the coast, where even now he was an outsider who never would be fully trusted, who had to get the selectmen's approval for the most trivial move. And now, even that tenuous hold seemed to be threatened by this red-haired scarecrow of a federal agent.

"To know that I am not investigating you," Ryan finished. He saw the adrenaline rush into Ghent's face, his mouth hanging open and his nostrils flaring. Ghent swayed back and forth on his feet, as if drunk. "Did you hear me?" Ryan said, not sure if Ghent was comprehending. "I was saying that my mission here—"

"Oh no?" Ghent shouted, even though he was barely two feet away from Ryan. "Well, then, fuck you!" And he took a giant roundhouse swing at Ryan.

In any normal situation, Ryan would have ducked or stepped back. But he was still partially shrouded in grief as he tried to piece together his new life. In that fog, all he did was throw up an arm to ward it off. When the fist glanced off his forearm, he staggered backward a step or two and was tripped by a fire hydrant, one of only two in the town, at either end of the business district. Ghent looked down at him, then turned and walked away, muttering, "Fuckety fuckety fuckety fuck." Now he had an assault on a federal official to add to his list of worries.

Ryan stood up, brushed himself off. Across the street he saw several faces staring out at him through the big plate glass window at the front of the Fisherman's Pal. The talk would be all over town in minutes. Then he continued his walk until he reached, at the western end of Main Street, the town's boatyard. He noticed his arm didn't hurt, so he figured it must mainly have been astonishment that knocked him off balance.

DINNER WITH PEELED PAUL

R yan strolled into the boatyard and wandered around its retail store. The prices of brass fittings for yachts amazed him. Four dollars for one three-inch screw, seventy-seven dollars for a brass door hinge. He recalled the old saying about yachts: "If you have to ask how much it costs, you can't afford it."

As he was heading out of the store, he saw a sign behind the cashier advertising the yard's boat rentals. They had two on hand, she told him: a big double-masted Concordia yawl for $1,500 a day, and a little Cape Dory Typhoon for $400 a day. On an impulse, he asked for the Typhoon.

"You know how to sail, right?" the cashier asked.

"Yep," he said. "But mainly on the West Coast. And I was in the navy."

The Typhoon, a twenty-foot sloop with a big one-ton keel, was perfect for these deep, cold waters. Because of the heavy bottom, it was almost impossible to capsize—important in an area where a person in the water would not last long before the frigid ocean current flowing down from Newfoundland would induce lethal hypothermia. The Typhoon was a plodder, with a maximum hull speed of about 6.5 knots. But that slowness also made it forgiving of human error. It wasn't like a racing boat that could poke its bow deep into the side of a cabin cruiser while the skipper was still trying to figure out how to slacken his sail.

Ryan motored from the marina's dock. When he reached the open water of the harbor, he raised the jib and mainsail. A light wind gently nudged him past the near islands. When he was out of their lees and fully exposed to the day's growing south-westerly breeze, the boat seemed to sense the change and come alive. The wind from the southwest picked up from 8 knots to about 15. As the mainsail bulged out, the hull leaned over to twenty degrees, the rail just above the water churning by, and the boat hit its maximum speed. Ryan could feel the energy in the tense "sheets," the lines that controlled the set of the mainsail and the jib. He sat up on the edge of the boat, holding the tiller extension, his feet down on the cockpit seats. He could sense a vibration, almost a happy humming, not just in the rigging, but in the mast and spars. The boat was telling him, *This is precisely what I was made for.*

Ryan let the boat go where it wanted, which, by happenstance, was southeast. It was exhilarating but also exhausting, something he didn't really notice. He was entirely absorbed, learning to control the boat with its rudder and sails. But he was also paying close attention to the world around him—open sea with some islands in the distance to his left—and what was underneath him in the sea bottom, which was uneven along the Maine coast, with deep holes and sudden ridges. These in turn played havoc with tides, which might be flowing in one direction in one spot and the opposite a mile later.

For two hours, the happy Typhoon scooted as best it could across the sparkling surface of the sea. Ryan realized he was nearing Ricky Cutts's fishing grounds, which, had he been honest with himself, might be what he had intended to do after all. But, he could counter, he hadn't set the wind that day to be perfect to send him to this spot. That was happenstance, he could plead.

He checked the boat's tiny GPS reader. It was a modern miracle, he thought, that something using six little AA batteries could reach out and collect multiple satellite signals and use them to determine and track his exact location on the earth's surface. How captains navigated the tides and seas and through the fogs before the existence of GPS was beyond him.

He was nearing Little Bold, with Big Bold in the distance. As he did, a great wave of fatigue rolled over him, not unlike a heavy sea fog that takes a boat from glittering brightness to abysmal shadows in a few moments. He felt like the sugar low was hitting him again. Or maybe it was a potassium crash induced by his poor diet. A few bananas weren't going to undo months of near starvation.

Or was it because he was venturing for the first time into Ricky Cutts's waters? If anyone was ever fit to be a cold, eyeless, chain-rattling, restless ghost, it was Ricky, Ryan lazily mused to himself. He was too tired to think clearly. He was stiff from the two hours of intense sailing. He turned the tiller to tuck the boat into the lee of Little Bold. He needed to stop. He loosened the halyard on the main and lowered the sail. He was too tired to furl it, so he just stuffed it around the boom. He put his head down on it—that should keep the sail in place, he thought—and promptly fell asleep. He didn't even think to look for an anchor.

Not far to the east, Peeled Paul was checking his weirs to see what the tide had pushed in. Sometimes a strong wind combined with a higher-than-usual flow did strange things to fish. Halibuts are bottom feeders, but for some reason, today one had drifted into one of his catchments. It weighed perhaps fourteen pounds. Paul cornered it and netted it and began thinking about dinner.

As he did, he heard the distinct heavy thump of fiberglass knocking into rock in the near distance. Not heavily, not breaking through a hull, but just a *thump*, pause, *thump*. And again. He climbed up on the islet adjoining the weir and looked to the direction of the sound. There, about two hundred yards away, on the northern edge of the Devil's Garden, he saw a green-hulled sailboat. Something was clearly amiss—the person in the boat was not sitting up, and the sail was down, with its belly over the side, drifting in the water.

Paul walked back to his fish table, on a level area in the rocks on the west side of Big Bold. He covered the halibut with a small tarp and rocks to keep off the sunlight and ospreys, then rowed his little craft out to the sailboat. "Mister," he shouted as he neared the man with his head on the boom, but to no effect. "Hey, mister!"

He maneuvered his little craft even closer, tied his painter onto the Typhoon's port cleat, and leaned into the little sailboat to tap the man. "Hey, buddy!" he said, louder. "Wake up."

Ryan slowly lifted his head. Only then did he open his eyes. He saw before him what appeared to be a naked Native American, with long black hair and a wispy black beard, in a small rowboat well out to sea. He slowly shook his head. For all he knew this was a hallucination.

"Can you hear me?" Paul asked. The whisper of an accent said to Ryan that this was indeed a tribal Indian.

Ryan nodded. Paul waited. Finally, Ryan said groggily, "My name is Ryan. I am not sure where I am."

"You're in the Devil's Garden," Paul said.

Well, Ryan thought, *that can't be good.*

Paul continued, "Mister, you look sunburned, probably dehydrated. You got water?"

Ryan confessed that he had neglected to bring any.

Paul devised a plan. He would tow the Typhoon the short way over to Big Bold, where they would anchor her. Then he would take Paul ashore and get him into shape. "While I tow," Paul instructed, "pull in that sail, furl it and then tie it with your halyard. Then go below and find an anchor." He added, "I'm Paul, by the way."

Twenty minutes later, with that all done, and Ryan ashore, Paul directed Ryan to the rough chair next to the fish table and handed him a plastic jug of water. "It's from my spring," Paul said. "A little funky, but passable."

Ryan sipped. The water felt wonderful. It seemed to be trickling into his tired muscles, reviving them.

Paul worked on the halibut at the fish table, cutting two large filets, then cubing them. The guts and skin and leftovers he put into piles and then stuffed those into several bait bags. Lobsters love halibut as much as people do. He put the bait bags into a bucket of seawater.

Ryan slowly revived as he watched Paul work. He still felt foggy, uncertain of where he was or what he was doing. "Am I trespassing, being here?" he finally asked. "I mean, this is tribal land, isn't it?"

Paul turned to look at him. "Oh, no, I invited you. You are my guest!" He told Ryan he was going into the island's interior to collect some vegetables and herbs for dinner. He grew fiddleheads near the spring and had found wild thyme on the north shore of the island. "You sit here and recover." He handed Ryan some duck jerky. "Chew on that. Have more water."

Paul returned about a half hour later.

"What's the Devil's Garden?" Ryan asked.

"Over there, where I found you," Paul pointed. "There're three black basalt dikes running from Little Bold toward us. Right now it's high tide, so you can't see them. They're ancient lava that bubbled up between cracks in other rock about two hundred million years ago. Over those years, the surrounding rock has eroded away, leaving the basalt standing hard, tall, and sharp.

"Wait six hours, and man, you'll be amazed. The dikes will stand out. You get your boat wedged in among there on the low, you'd have a hell of a time getting it out. Even worse would be to be jammed across two of them."

"You seem to know your stuff," Ryan said, impressed at the geological summary.

"Used to be a high school teacher," Paul said, "until I wised up."

As the sun neared the western horizon, Paul lit a roaring fire of maple and oak and let it burn down to coals. He put a stack of fiddleheads in a pan on the edge of the fire. Then, when there was just some orange left in the western sky, it was time to eat. "Watch me," Paul said. He speared a white cube of the halibut on a willow stick. Then he dipped it in a bowl on the table containing a mix of oil and thyme. Then he held it over the coals, about one minute a side. Then he handed it to Ryan. It was, Ryan thought, the best fish he ever had eaten. He chewed slowly.

The conversation was slow and meandering in a pleasant way. No one needed to be anywhere, and there was nothing to do but eat, talk, and look at the stars beginning to shine. "Ryan, are you on vacation out here?" Paul asked, as he prepared his own cube and placed it above the coals.

"You don't know what I'm doing here?" Ryan said. "Everyone else does."

"No," Paul said. "You see, I'm pretty isolated out here. Just meet someone from the Malpense Island once a week." He explained how that had come to be, what had happened that day with Darla and then with his father, how he had been sentenced to a year's isolation on the island, and finally decided to stay. "I like it," he said.

It was a simple seaside feast. They each ate more halibut. They passed the fiddlehead pan back and forth. Those vegetables were chewy but bursting with nutrition. Paul had salted them with sea salt he had made himself the previous winter, in the continuously bubbling pot over his cabin fire.

Ryan considered Paul's account of how he had come to this island. "Your situation is not unlike my own," Ryan said slowly, as much to himself as to Paul. He stared at the coals in the fire as they alternated from red to black. He said that a family disaster had propelled him to this remote spot here on a rock slope on an island in the Atlantic Ocean. He recounted the previous seven months of his life. He had been an FBI agent assigned to San Diego, he said. Paul listened and nodded.

When Ryan said that his wife and two children had died, Paul quickly stood, turned toward the half-moon hanging on the southeastern horizon, and said a short prayer in Malpense. Then he turned back to face Ryan. "And now you're FBI here?" he said.

"Yes," Ryan said. "I'm investigating the Ricky Cutts situation."

"Ricky?" Paul was surprised. "Is he in trouble, like federal trouble?"

Ryan paused. This guy really didn't know? Ryan laughed inwardly. Finally, he had met someone who seemed to be as clueless as everyone thought Ryan was. "When was the last time you saw Ricky?" he finally asked. *This is a damned odd conversation*, he thought.

"Not sure," Paul said. "About two weeks ago, I saw Ricky's boat, about a mile over there"—he pointed west—"when a lobster boat out of Liberty pulled up to it. No more than a couple of minutes. Figured someone dropping off a part or a tool. It wasn't Topsail," he said, referring to the fisherman who worked the waters adjoining Ricky's on the west. "His hull is green. This one was white. Might have been one of the Highliners—it was a good boat."

And then?

"Funny thing was, the white boat pulled away, but there didn't seem to be anyone at the helm on Ricky's boat. That's why I say I know I saw Ricky's boat, with that stupid name, but I am not sure I saw Ricky that day. His boat just drifted along to the north."

"You weren't worried?" Ryan asked.

"Nah," he said. "Ricky might have been below working on the engine. Or, knowing him, sleeping one off." Paul hadn't given it much thought and had gone about his business elsewhere on the island.

"You didn't think of checking on him, like you did with me?"

Paul shook his head. "With you, today, I took one look at you with your sail in the water and thought, *That guy's in distress.* And it was just a five-minute row to go and help you. With Ricky, I'm not going to row out half an hour out just to get insulted. He'd probably say, 'Fuck you, red man, and stay out of my traps.' He's not a nice guy."

"Did you tell anyone what you saw?"

"I have a job as a watchman for the tribe. So yeah, I told Sub-chief Johnny Mac, over on Malpense."

"And?"

Paul stopped. He didn't like talking about tribal ways with outsiders. "Kind of gave me the Indian eye roll," he said softly.

"Which means?"

Paul said, even more softly, almost imperceptibly, "He didn't have to say it, but I got the message that we stay out of Anglo foolishness, and we keep them out of ours. That is the best way." Both Paul and Johnny Mac knew the story, handed down from parent to child, of how on a Sunday in November 1965, five hunters from Massachusetts had barged onto the Pleasant Point Reservation in eastern Maine, home of several hundred Passamaquoddy

Indians. They were looking to buy alcohol and sex. After getting two cases of beer but not access to women, they attacked a member of the tribe, beating him to death with a piece of lumber. The local police didn't investigate thoroughly, the county prosecutor bungled the case, and the one hunter who was charged was found not guilty by a local all-White jury.

Ryan was intrigued. "Johnny Mac didn't tell you Ricky was dead, had been killed out there?"

"No," Paul said. "I wonder why. Probably just keeping us out of it." He was quiet a long time and then looked up from the fire. "You sure he's dead?"

"Yes," Ryan said. "Seen the body, in fact. Twice. Pulled him out of the water over on Isle au Haut."

Paul nodded and stood again to face the moon. He uttered the short prayer for the dead for the second time that evening. He picked up the fish table's top and took it down to the water to rinse it off. He came back up and replaced it. He seemed pensive, adding up in his mind everything they had talked about over their meal. "It is strange," he said. "I think we are two men who each have gone through hells of sorts, been chased by demons. Yet here we are, on the edge of a kind of paradise, a Maine island on a fine summer evening."

"I am glad you have found peace," Ryan said, sensing that it was time to go.

"I hope you do too," Paul responded. He threw a bucket of water over the remains of the fire. They carried the rowboat down to the water's edge. He gave Ryan a ride out to the anchored sailboat. Ryan, feeling enormously better from the water, the meal, and the conversation, climbed aboard. Paul handed him a gallon jug of his spring water, "for your trip home tomorrow." They shook hands. Ryan told Paul that if he ever needed a favor, to please let him know. Paul nodded. Ryan watched Paul row up around the north end of Big Bold and disappear around the curve of the shore.

It had been a long day, from Bangor, to Abby Buck, to the call with Louise, the odd encounter with Ghent, and then the sail out to Little Bold, and finally his encounter with Paul. Ryan lay down in the cockpit of the boat, using the spare jib for a blanket. He fell asleep looking at the sky overhead and the occasional shooting star. The meteors for some reason made him think about the attraction he felt toward Solid Harrison, despite meeting her just once for about fifteen minutes. It was the first time he had thought about sex in a long, long time. He fell into a deep sleep.

When he awoke ten hours later, it was silent and quiet, just after low tide. He sat up in the cockpit and looked over at the Devil's Garden, a mere hundred yards south of his anchorage. At this tide, with the water twelve feet lower than when he had drifted in yesterday near high tide, it looked too close for comfort, a nautical jagged version of Stonehenge, black slabs of rock angled upward, running in three parallel lines out from Little Bold. He realized that he had been very lucky that Paul had been in the neighborhood to awaken him and tow his boat out of there.

A seal surfaced, wondering what this boat was doing in his hunting grounds. Ryan said, "Hello." The animal, unpersuaded, dove. Ryan had used muscles yesterday that hadn't been exercised in a long time. His arms felt too stiff to sail, so he pulled on the starter cord of the Typhoon's little long-shaft six-horsepower Yamaha outboard and chugged northwestward for a few hours.

At the boatyard store he paid his bill—$400 for less than twenty-four hours. He pointed out to the cashier that he had put some scratches on the hull. He said he was happy to pay to have them painted. "No worries," the cashier said. "We expect that on the small rentals." She assured him that the boys in the paint shop would slap on some paint, "just like they take care of me." He wasn't sure exactly what she meant with that dollop of Maine humor, so he thanked her and left.

THE VIEW FROM ECHO LAKE

He checked in with Harriet. "Are you following Doc Healey's orders to take time off?" she asked.

"Yep. Went sailing yesterday. Going hiking today." What he didn't say was that he needed time to digest what he had learned from Abby, Louise, and Peeled Paul. Whose white boat had visited Ricky Cutts down near Big Bold? How to find out more?

"Harriet, did you ever have a case where it just didn't make sense?"

She considered that for a moment, going through memories of her earlier cases in Miami and then in Portland. "Not really," she said. "Pretty much all of them, in the end, the bad guy was motivated by one of the seven deadly sins." She paused. "Well, not gluttony, that I can remember."

"What about sloth?" he asked.

"That's easy," she said. "We always say criminals are stupid, but I think a lot are just flat-out lazy. They're always looking for shortcuts. So sloth is a biggie, really." He thanked her and promised to stay in touch.

Once back on the mainland, he gassed up and went into the adjoining Walgreens to pick up the potassium pills that he should have taken yesterday. He drove to Acadia National Park on Mount Desert Island. On the way, he tried to remember all seven of those sins. Indeed, most of the cases he'd seen involved the big three: greed, lust, and wrath. Sloth, okay, if you buy Harriet's interpretation. Envy and pride, those were harder to nail down. But what if Abby Buck was right, that he should be looking not at deadly sins but at deadly virtues?

He had expected a national park area to be bucolic. Entering Bar Harbor, he was taken aback by the backup of cars and buses. He hadn't seen a traffic jam like that since coming to Maine. Cars lining up to buy gas. Cars waiting for parking spaces. Cars that just had nowhere to go. Tour buses idling. A cruise ship moored offshore had disgorged over one thousand passengers, who swarmed the sidewalks, restaurants, and knickknack stores. He decided to drive over to "the quiet side" of the island, on the southwest part, far from Bar Harbor. There, almost randomly, he saw a sign for a trailhead at the south end of Echo Lake.

He enjoyed the strain of clambering up the boulder-strewn cliff on the west side of the lake. His leg muscles felt more alive than they had in months. Perhaps physical strain eased mental anguish, balanced it somehow. Halfway up he encountered a young park ranger sitting on a rock, likely there to ensure that hikers' dogs were properly leashed. The ranger noticed the ankle holster and asked why he had it. All in two strides, Ryan told her he was federal law enforcement "on vacation," showed her his wallet badge, and kept going. She frowned at his coldness. But he wasn't in the mood for another jibe about being the FBI guy exiled to Bangor, even though she looked like a summer intern who probably wouldn't be in on that joke. "Be careful of sunburn!" she admonished up the trail behind him.

He needed to be alone with his thoughts. He was mulling what Louise had said. The girls didn't kill their father. They didn't know who did. But. But. He pondered her word "grateful." And Paul definitely had seen a Liberty lobster boat approach Ricky Cutts's boat, a white one. The trail grew steeper. He hunched forward and tried to maintain his speed. His legs ached a bit. He was grateful for the exercise, for the chance to push himself physically.

He finally reached the summit of Beech Mountain. He was rewarded with far-reaching views to the east and south offering that ideal combination of green mountains rising out of the blue sea. He followed the trail northward along the flat top of the cliff. Near an old fire tower, he noticed a side path that led to an outcropping of the cliff, tucked behind some dwarf pines, even smaller than usual because of their exposed location and rocky soil. He settled down to drink in the view, leaning back against granite that had been warmed by the sun. He looked out over Sargent Mountain to the east, its long horizontal patches of bald gray rock highlighted by the afternoon sun. Just behind Sargent, a sliver of its near-twin, Cadillac Mountain, peeked over.

As he surveyed the fine view, he began summarizing all he had learned. Drugs had been promising, but had amounted to—really, not much. The fish market angle also appeared to be a dead end. In both cases, there was money involved, lots of it. But nothing that pointed to a desire or need to kill. Rather the opposite: every indication was that Cutts's murder had been an unwelcome disruption, one that bothered people in part because they didn't understand it. That told him that the action did not fit into their worlds.

Then there was that woman at the shelter. She was telling him something, but he wasn't sure what—it looked like the girls had been abused but had no part in the killing, and certainly no foreknowledge that would make them accomplices. Why had Johnny Mac, the Malpense subchief, not told him about a white boat visiting Ricky Cutts? And Abby Buck's mocking seemed to contain a kernel of truth. Add it all up, and? It was as if the island and its culture were one organic entity, as the rude spy had indicated. How to analyze it?

At Quantico, a veteran instructor had taught a novel investigative technique. Frustration is not a bad symptom, he had counseled. Sometimes it builds when you are on the verge of figuring out something, but don't know what it is. "At that point," he had instructed, "you need to stand back a bit. Frustration can be how your subconscious signals that it is onto something. When that happens, get out of your office, be alone, find a spot of nature where you can meditate. First, concentrate on a distant sight—the moon, say, or a faraway hill. Even a single tree across a field will do. Do that for a while, and let the subconscious have its way. Then focus on something closer—a leaf or flower or bug.

"When you feel calm and centered, you're ready," the instructor had continued. "Ask yourself probing questions, especially the uncomfortable ones we usually let ourselves avoid. Bring the subconscious to the surface. Begin with, 'What is my greatest fear?' Contemplate that seriously, most especially when you want to drop it. Then, when you feel you have a genuine answer, move to the next one—which should be easier now: 'What is my greatest fear about this investigation?'"

Ryan put it into practice now. He focused on Great Cranberry Island, off to the southeast, and on the bright white sails of boats moving around it. He did not move. He reminded himself to notice every aspect of the environment: The slight wind out of the south ruffling the hair on his arms, more on his right than his left. The slightly greater pressure from the wind on his right ear. The pine branches lifting slightly. The way the spruce and fir trees in the distance appeared grayer and bluer than the green ones near him. And back to the islands, to the sails. The slow flight of clouds, their movement perceivable only if compared to the stationary tree branches. The shadows of the clouds darkening patches of the ocean's surface. The sun's rightward arc on its daily journey. The occasional shouts of swimmers and canoeists drifting up faintly from the lake far below, sounding almost like memories of earlier summers.

The questions rose, and the self-interrogation began.

What, currently, is your greatest fear? *Losing my mind, collapsing entirely, falling into the vortex of grief.*

Wait. Wait.

Eventually. Let out your breath. What is your biggest worry about this investigation? *That I am being made a fool.*

Wait. Why is that? *Because someone or something is indeed fooling me.* He was surprised that the answer, when it finally came, was so crystal clear.

And what had made him think of the tourists yesterday at the harbor as chumps? This time the volume of the voice in the back of his head rose slightly. *Because you are one too.*

What did that mean? It meant he was no different from those tourists, looking only at the superficial. Abby Buck's phrase floated up to him, almost crawling up the cliff: "Everyone on this island." It seemed to echo in his mind, as if the water in the lake far below him was talking. "Everyone on this island knows." What was below the surface? What was on the surface? How were those two things different?

He stood to stretch. His leg muscles complained. Out of nowhere, the reading in the island church of the passage from Luke came back to him: *It were better for him that a millstone were hanged about his neck, and he cast into the sea, than that he should offend one of these little ones. Take heed to yourselves: If thy brother trespass against thee, rebuke him. . . .*

If you've been playing poker for half an hour? Who was the guide for the patsy, the one leading him along the path? Who was steering his understanding, explaining every step of the way? As he picked his way back down the cliff, the voice in the back of his head delivered a verdict: *It is time to talk to Caleb again.* Who had driven that white boat to confront Ricky Cutts west of Big Bold?

But it really will be the first time I've talked to Caleb, Ryan said inwardly back to that nettlesome voice. He gave a small wave to the young ranger as he passed her again. He wondered if this leash-checking assignment was some sort of punishment for a work screwup. *Now, Agent Tapia, you're thinking like a Mainer*, he chuckled to himself.

Getting in his truck, he thought to himself: *Either Caleb did it, or he knows who did. And if it wasn't him, it was Herc.* How to figure out the answer to that? He mulled it over on the hour-long drive up Route 1A back to the west side of Bangor.

By the time he was home, he had a plan in mind. For the first time in the Cutts investigation, he felt like he had caught up with what was going on. He developed some follow-up questions. Following Harriet's admonition and Healey's orders, he did some grocery shopping and ate a big salad for dinner. But even as he chewed, he thought that it was a far cry from the halibut feast of the previous evening.

A CONVERSATION OVER TEA

Early Monday morning he drove down through the darkness to Liberty's harbor, dutifully eating four bananas as he drove. For the first time, he parked on the commercial wharf—unaware that he was violating an actual written rule that only commercial fishermen could do that—and waited for Caleb to appear. To the lobstermen gathering for the day, his truck's unusual presence in their lot made a statement, whether he realized it or not. He sat in the cab and waited. As the day dawned, he looked over Liberty's lobster boats on their moorings: About thirty-five were visible from his spot on the wharf. Some had black hulls, others green and red. Two yellow, and one blue—not a favored color among mariners. And perhaps fifteen white hulls. He stared at those, one by one. *Which one?* he asked himself.

Just before five in the morning, Caleb's pickup rolled onto the wharf. Below its Maine license plate, featuring a red lobster, hung a smaller plate that stated "VFD." In Maine, this meant that the driver was a volunteer firefighter. But to locals, it signified also that the driver was a standup guy who took time to help neighbors, usually more with directing traffic around car crashes than with house fires.

Caleb talked briefly to the Highliners, who were nodding toward Ryan. He then walked over to Ryan and said, "Agent Tapia." It was both a greeting and a question.

Ryan asked for permission to come aboard the *Sea Angel*. "Of course," Caleb said, always low-key, even, and gracious. And, it being Maine, he added, "Heard about your prize fight. From-aways getting in street brawls, gonna give Liberty a bad name."

Ryan shot back, "Damn, what did you all talk about before I came to town?"

Caleb chuckled—that had been the proper Maine riposte. Ryan stepped down into the handsome white lobster boat. He was focused today. He asked to see the *Sea Angel*'s tool kit.

"May I ask why?" Caleb said, with slightly raised eyebrows.

"Just to help me understand something in my investigation," Ryan said, not being completely candid. "I'm interested in the working tools of the lobsterman."

Caleb shrugged, went below, and brought up the long blue toolbox. Even for his muscled biceps, it was heavy. He hefted it onto the main deck with two hands and placed it before Ryan.

Ryan flipped up the two black clasps and opened the top. The tools were all there, in their proper places. Gazing at them brought back his days as a navy engineman. From left to right, there were crimpers, strippers, hose clamps, a hose cutter, scissors, a short hacksaw, duct tape, a hammer, channel-lock pliers, a complete set of smaller pliers, two sets of screwdrivers, two sets of ratcheting wrenches (both metric and American), spare fuel filters, a jimmy, a sandwich bag of various fuses and, of course, a magnetic clawed retriever, for retrieving tools and screws dropped in the bilge. The tools were clean. All but one carried the nicks and marks of being used. Even with care and being wiped down after every use with an oilcloth, most bore the unmistakable brown spotting that is the fate of all tools kept aboard a saltwater boat, even supposedly stainless steel.

Just one tool was unspotted: in the middle, where the heaviest of the tools were stored, shone the bright silvery metal of a brand-new, never-used pipe wrench, what landlubbers would call a "monkey wrench." Caleb would not leave the dock without one, not while helming a lobster boat powered by an aging Cummins engine. So much could go wrong at sea—coolant loss, a blown head gasket, a clogging impeller that would make an engine overheat in minutes. Ryan asked himself: *What had happened recently that made Caleb need a new wrench?*

Ryan looked up at Caleb. "Nice wrench." He waited. "Brand new wrench," he added, unnecessarily but pointedly. Until that moment he hadn't known whether he should focus on Herc or Caleb. Now he knew.

"And?" Caleb asked.

Ryan left that question hanging in the air. Instead, he asked if Caleb ever looked at overhead imagery of these waters. "Of course," the lobsterman said. "The satellite shots are interesting, but I haven't found them particularly useful for lobstering." As he spoke, doubt crossed his face, as if to ask, *Where are you going with this?* It was the first time Ryan had seen Caleb on the back foot.

"Well," Ryan said, "on the day Ricky Cutts was killed, around the time when the medical examiner has determined that his skull was struck twice, there's an image of another boat coming in at his." Ryan was bluffing but was betting that Caleb had no way of knowing that. The federal government had all sorts of assets that Ryan might have accessed. *I've peered into your toolbox, but you haven't seen mine*, Ryan thought.

"Oh?" said Caleb. His hand went to his chin. He seemed at a loss for the first time since Ryan had met him.

Ryan pressed his attack. "Why didn't you go to the wake for Ricky?"

Caleb stood and paced the short way up and down his deck, from wheelhouse to stern. Ryan said nothing. He could wait. He did. He was tired of being the dummy, always one step behind everyone else on this island. He thought, *Your move, Caleb*. Another technique his mentor had taught: oftentimes, silence is the best question.

Uncertainty played on Caleb's face. He seemed lost in thought. Finally, after two or three minutes, he looked at Ryan and said, "Want some tea?"

Buying time? Ryan wondered. He turned over that thought and dismissed it. He decided instead that Caleb was just considering his presentation, finalizing thoughts that had been in his head for some time.

Ryan waited, looking over the dawning day. Few things are so ripe with anticipation as a lobster fleet gearing up for the day's work, a combination of energy and competence as dozens of boat engines warm up and scores of fishermen ready themselves. Even the gulls were getting in place, ready to fly behind the boats of the more generous skippers, those who might toss them small fish found in traps.

Caleb appeared from below with two mugs of tea and sat down on the gunwale opposite Ryan. "Agent Tapia, I think you know why I didn't go to Ricky's farewell that day," he said. But then he stopped talking.

Ryan finally said, "Yes, but I want you to tell me."

Caleb sat and sipped his tea. Then he said, "I want you to know—I never lied to you."

"Not sure what you mean by that," Ryan said.

"It means," Caleb said, "that I always told you the truth, as I understand it." He paused. "For you, I think, it isn't a job that drives you, it's a sense of duty."

Ryan nodded. "Yes. I signed up to protect people."

Caleb nodded in turn. "Me too. It's just a different community I try to protect. But a sense of duty." He halted again, as if he had said what he wanted to say.

Ryan waited. *I think he is ready to tell me,* he thought to himself. "So," he said, "why kill Ricky?" A lot depended on what Caleb said next. He waited.

Caleb's voice slowed to a crawl. His blue eyes looked straight at Ryan. "Had to." Pause. He pursed his lips. "No choice." Pause. Shook his head slowly.

"That's it?" Ryan said. He thought, *Jesus, what did that even mean?*

Caleb revived a bit and looked up. "Aren't you supposed to give me a Miranda warning, something like that?" he asked. He seemed curious about how this was going to go, but not about how it was going to end.

"No," Ryan said. "Not necessary. I think you're going to write out a full confession before the day is over. Right now, I just want to understand what happened."

Caleb was, in fact, eager to talk. It had been building inside him. Ryan stared at him. Caleb did not have the hangdog look like a man caught for the act of murder. Rather, he seemed to have a righteous glow on his face, of steeled determination. He was, Ryan realized, proud of what he had done. It had been his duty as one of the leading men on the island. Not a pleasant one, Caleb might say, but duty rarely is. Duty is not what you want to do, it is what you have to do, even if no one else is around. It is the price of position and status, Caleb believed. And the hardest part of it is deciding what must be done when no one is there to tell you what to do. Caleb had seen his duty, and he had done it.

Caleb's account came pouring out. The fatal days had begun when he was out fishing one afternoon in late May, just over two weeks earlier. "The traps were just giving me onesies and twosies, nothing great," he recalled. "Barely cover the cost of bait and fuel. I could see a thick fog rolling in from the south, so I turned back up the bay. On the way back to Liberty I decided to take a deer, at least have something to show for the day's work.

"I landed on the sand on a small island where lately I'd seen a few big does. The fog was just catching up with me. I was making my way quietly, locating the herd, walking softly on a mossy animal path, when I heard what first seemed to be the shriek of a child."

He looked at Ryan. "Thought it must be an osprey or bald eagle, likely badly wounded, maybe with a wing torn by a badger or fox. That sound crawls right up your back and freezes you. Hard to tell where it was coming from, because sounds bounce around in the fog. So I was looking around for a bird that maybe got caught on the ground. I heard that banshee cry again. This time it was higher. And closer. Sounded almost like a woman wailing.

"I dropped down to a crouch, behind a spruce on the edge of the meadow on the southern shore of the island. I looked through its branches. Heard the scream again. And then I like to vomited."

"What was it?" Ryan asked.

"I could only see his back, his bare ass, white as a full moon, but I knew right away it was Ricky Cutts. His pants down around his ankles. Had his daughter, the little one with the purple hair, bent forward in front of him over a boulder in the meadow, her pants down too." There, in the wisps of fog and long green grass, a scene of horror.

He paused and shook his head slowly. "And he was, uh, fucking her from behind. He had a knot of her hair wrapped around his right hand, all purple you know, and he was yanking it, pulling her head back up. I could see her face a bit. He was pushing into her, yelling all the time, 'Bitch, bitch, bitch. I'll show you, bitch.'"

"You had your rifle, and you're a crack shot," Ryan observed. "Why didn't you shoot him?"

"Yep," he nodded. "My first thought. Even raised the barrel and took my aim. Fifty, sixty feet. Easy shot. I could squat, get down to a firing angle where I could take off the back of his head without the round passing through and hitting her. I felt for the trigger." His eyes narrowed at the memory, his body remembering the squint and the automatic stopping of breath before taking a shot.

"And then I thought, what am I going to do, splatter his brains all over her? And then have her explain to the world what happened?" Caleb shuddered. "Last thing that poor girl needs."

"So?"

"Sooo," Caleb said quietly, elongating the word, as he considered the path he had then pursued. "I backed quietly out, back to that animal track, moved slowly to the woods back to the beach where I'd left the *Sea Angel*. I pushed it off, didn't turn on the engine, let her drift southward on the tide for about half an hour. When it carried us behind another little island, I fired up the engine, chugged away slowly."

He concluded, "As for Ricky, I don't think he ever suspected in the least he had been seen."

Ryan was still puzzling it through. "If you had shot him at that moment you saw him raping her, no jury would have convicted you of murder. At worse, some reduced charge."

Anger and exasperation reddened Caleb's face. "Too damn bad I didn't bring my lawyer with me that day."

Ryan took a breath. He realized that Caleb had been over that moment again and again in his head, second-guessing himself. Maybe he could have yelled, gotten Ricky to step away, and then shot him.

Ryan's comment had been a misstep, coming across as querulous. He sipped his tea. Waited. He said, "So instead, you let things simmer for a couple of days, then took your boat down to where you knew he'd be fishing?"

"You got it," Caleb confessed. "It was simple." He began thinking it over as he steered his boat back to town. He saw then what he was required to do. Two mornings later, he drove his boat out and pulled some traps, keeping the robin fish, sculpin, and other small swimmers that he found in them, instead of throwing them to the gulls, as he usually would. He cut them up into a bucket, which then held a bloody mess. "Then I gunned the *Angel* across the bay southeast to his fishing grounds, saw his boat, hitched onto one of his cleats, and stepped over the gunwale," he said, pronouncing the last word as "gunnel."

Caleb was reliving the moment. "I came in fast. He saw me, slowly focused on me, was still figuring out what I wanted. All in the same move I stepped onto his deck, I brought my pipe wrench straight down on his skull, hard, even as he stared at me. Real hard. It felt good. His eyes bulged out real hard, and then he crumpled. When he was down, I raised up high and swung the wrench again, even harder, to make sure he stayed there."

Caleb was staring across the harbor, but what he was seeing in his mind was Ricky Cutts lying dead at his feet. "I was surprised at how fast and easy the whole thing was."

Ryan said, "And then you made it look like he got entangled in his gear, pulled out the stern by a trap?"

"Yeah," said Caleb, "that was the idea. Happens to someone every couple of years—guy's foot gets caught in a loop of a rope attached to a trap he's tossing, out the end he goes. If he's fishing alone and the boat's engine is engaged, end of story." A sloppy mariner like Ricky Cutts, maybe working half-drunk, would be a natural victim of such an accident. "After running the line twice around Ricky's ankles in an easy hitch, I hosed down the deck with salt water, then poured out the bloody bait bucket over it, hosed again, then shifted Ricky's engine to a notch above idle, and slid the body off the stern. Then I let his boat go, pointed north, making maybe three knots, enough to counter the tide." The whole thing took less than five minutes from tying up to Ricky's boat to pulling away.

And so you cast him into the sea for his offense against a little one, Ryan thought. And the churchmen approved. "But why send his boat toward Malpense?"

Caleb shook his head. "That was sheer accident," he said. "The boat was supposed to drag his body behind on the buoy rope. But the goddamn floating rope was built to part, to prevent right whales from lethal entanglements. So at some point, when the tension suddenly increased, probably from wave action, the rope snapped." At that point the *Pussy Man* and its dead skipper went their separate ways.

"He floated north, his boat curved to the east. I had assumed the southerly winds would push the boat back up into the bay. That's good because his girls could use the money from selling it." Instead, the neglected vessel had shrugged off the wind and ridden an eastward current eddying off the Gulf of Maine. "Maybe the rudder pulled over. Or could be he was so slovenly in his boat keeping that he hadn't cleaned his hull in months. Probably had kelp four feet long hanging from the bottom."

Ryan looked blank and gave a slight shake of his head.

Caleb explained, "With the weeds hanging off a hull like that, it adds drag, which makes it more prone to be pushed by current than by wind. Anyway, it wound up out on Malpense, and that led you down the wrong path."

"Okay," Ryan said. "But why would the subchief out there want me to think drugs were involved in Ricky Cutts's getting killed?"

Caleb shrugged. "You got me. Might have seen my boat out near Ricky's and was trying to do me a favor."

That response raised a new set of questions, but Ryan ignored them. As Harriet had made clear, nothing good could come from turning over rocks on Malpense Island. And right now, he needed to keep the focus on the events immediately surrounding the death of Ricky Cutts.

"So," Ryan asked, "what happened to the pipe wrench?" The toolbox sat open on the deck between them, almost accusatory.

"I tossed it in Champlain's Hole," Caleb said. "Out where the Malpense catch their sturgeon." That was consistent of him. Many lobstermen would have simply dropped the wrench overboard any-where, but not fastidious Caleb, Ryan thought—he would go the extra step and motor to a spot where it would drop sixty fathoms, making it almost impossible to find.

Caleb looked at Ryan. "Hey, am I allowed to ask you a question?"

"Sure," said Ryan.

"Why did you want to see my toolbox just now?" Caleb asked. He was genuinely interested.

Give him the respect, Ryan thought. "Because you take pride in your work and your vessel," he replied. "A skipper like you wouldn't let his boat leave the dock without a good pipe wrench."

"So me getting a brand new one—that was the sign that you needed that I was your man?" Caleb asked.

Yep, Ryan nodded.

"Done in by my own fussiness," Caleb sighed.

"Yep. But, to your credit, you expected to get away with it, I think," Ryan said.

Caleb nodded this time. He looked down at his tea, then out across the home harbor he knew he was about to leave. "Matter of fact, yes, I did. I thought the body would be found along with the boat, drifting in the bay. The county's busy. State Troopers investigate, chalk it up to maritime mishap. Happens all the time. Couple of days in the water, bouncing off the rocks, body's too chewed up by the fish and crabs to show much."

"What if they noticed the head wound?"

"Worst case, if they figured out it was inflicted, they would find out what you found—that almost anyone could have killed Ricky Cutts. Not really a case you want to invest a lot of time and money in, with other crimes out there, and community pressure to get to them. People here hate the New Yorkers driving dope up the turnpike."

Caleb looked up at Ryan. "So I had cosmic bad luck," he said. "You know what that is like, I suspect, with you losing your family. I am sorry for that. Hell of a thing to go through."

Yes, I do have a sense of cosmic bad luck, Ryan thought. He didn't realize Caleb knew about the accident. Caleb noticed the surprise on his face. "After you talked to Abby Buck the first time, he hired some business research outfit down in Washington, DC, to figure out who you were, make sure you really weren't DEA or something," Caleb said. "Abby likes to know who he is dealing with. He's smart that way." Within twenty-four hours, the research firm had sent back a dossier that included printouts of articles that had appeared in the San Diego *Union-Tribune* and the *East County Californian* the previous December about the deaths of the FBI man's wife and children in a truck-automobile collision on Jamacha Road. "Abby's shy of me, so he gave it to the harbormaster, knowing he'd share it with me, and I read it right here one morning." He looked around the boat's deck.

"Some of that cosmic bad luck landed on me, I guess," Caleb said, spreading his hands apart. "First, it was just a fluke that Ricky washed up on federal land. And second, even worse, his boat drifted over to Indian shores. And shit, you know, third, to top it off, suddenly I have a depressed FBI man with nothing else on his plate and all the time in the world to wander around my island asking questions."

Caleb looked at Ryan. "That was not the scenario I had counted on," he said. "Over the last week, I felt sometimes like it was some kind of bad karma, both of us being widowed young."

Ryan blurted out, "I never dream about Marta and Pablo and Stefanie being alive, only dead or about to be." He surprised himself by saying it. The words tumbled out of him. It seemed to be a day for revelations. "I don't know why. I wish I could envision them alive." He sensed tears welling up in his eyes. Somehow, they felt good. "Even Peaches. She was our dog."

Caleb considered that thought, his arms folded over his chest. He nodded in sympathy. "I'd say you're stuck in that moment." He added, "Maybe that's why I had to go after Ricky Cutts, otherwise I would be stuck in that moment of seeing him raping Lizzy. I needed to erase that. I've known that girl since she was a toddler."

Ryan was struck that in those four sentences, Caleb had changed roles. He was no longer a confessor. Rather, he was reverting to his familiar position in the community as a sympathetic and knowledgeable counselor.

Ryan had one last question: "But why did it have to be you who did it?"

Caleb looked at him in surprise. He thought the answer was obvious. "If not me, who else? The man had to be stopped. And I was the one who witnessed his crime. Keep it simple, do it fast and clean." To him, it was a simple matter of self-respect. "A man addresses the challenges life throws at him," he said. "If you can't, then hang it up and move into the nursing home."

"That's vigilante justice," Ryan said. "In the real world, we call the police. That's the deal. In a nation of laws, we don't get to be judge, jury, and executioner."

Goodwin waved a hand dismissively. "Sure. I considered that before I went down there to his fishing grounds. Say I reported seeing a rape. Maybe the Hancock County deputies find the evidence of his crime. And maybe they don't. Probably not. Maybe with all the gossip and outsiders stepping on her life, the raw details, Lizzy gets overwhelmed, feels dragged through the mud, police asking about her drug use like everything was her fault, and she gets fed up, kills herself. Or instead, maybe while all that plays out, she kills him and goes to jail. Or, best case, he winds up convicted of some lesser charge, does three or four years in Thomaston, comes back, and starts into his old ways, if not with those girls, with someone else." He said he had thought about this over and over again after what he saw on the little island. "There were no good answers. At least none I could see. The one I came up with, I think it was the least bad one."

And since Ryan had come to the island, Caleb had been thinking about explaining why he had done what he had done. He was speaking quickly now, using phrases he had been turning over in his mind for a week. "You call it vigilante," Caleb said. "Here's how I see it: I obeyed the laws of our fathers." He didn't quite say it, but in his view, and in the eyes of his neighbors, he had shouldered the burden and bore it well—as best he could. "The rest was just, well, bad luck," he said. "It happens. All the time."

He finished his tea and tried to slow himself down. "At some point, with a guy like Ricky Cutts, you have to step in and help out. Just put an end to it." The island had rules: *You do what you have to do, and then you carry the consequences. No one said life was fair.* Caleb didn't tell Ryan, but he figured that he'd likely wind up spending a few years behind bars in Thomaston. An island jury, if there were such a thing, wouldn't even charge him. A mainland jury, a bit more remote from the hard ways of the fishing life, would say blood requires punishment, and he needed to do some time. He could live with that. Maybe even get his bad knees worked on while he was in prison. His boat would be ready and his fishing grounds would be waiting for him when he got out. He was confident of that.

"Why did you go out of your way to be my guide on the island?" Ryan inquired.

"Again, same basic answer. Someone has to do it. And me doing it, that keeps the damage to a minimum. Fewer people involved—keeps it simple. And, of course, guiding you helped me keep tabs on you, on what you were asking about, and who you were looking at."

"That Ranger Goodwin, what was his role?" Ryan asked. "How was he trying to steer me for you?"

Puzzlement crossed Caleb's face for the first time in the conversation. "Who?" He was genuinely flummoxed. Then it dawned on him, and he laughed. "That park ranger over to Acadia, the dope smoker? You think he's involved?" He shook his head, amused by the thought. "I've met him maybe once or twice when he's on duty at Duck Harbor. Nothing to do with it. Maybe a second cousin. I've got relatives up and down this coast, a lot I've never met."

"Don't you think it's time to go?" Caleb said. He took the tea mugs, rinsed them, and stowed them in their place. He put away the toolbox that had tripped him up. He looked over the cabin one more time to make sure everything was Bristol fashion. He came back up to the deck, stood at the wheel, and ran his hands over it. Ryan realized he was bidding farewell to his boat and gave him the time he needed. After a spell, Caleb turned to Ryan and said, "I'm ready to go."

VOYAGES

t was indeed time. Ryan needed to get Caleb off the island quietly and into federal custody, many miles away. The tide had fallen about five feet while they talked. When they began, their heads had been a bit lower than the dock. Now they were well below it. To disembark the *Sea Angel* they had to climb a ladder up to the wharf.

Only then, as he ascended and stood on the dock, did Ryan see that knots of men had gathered. Ryan hadn't noticed that no lobster boats had gone out that morning. This was a significant morning in the lives of the island's fishing community. The men, and a few women who lobstered, had been waiting while Ryan and Caleb talked. They stood still as Ryan and Caleb walked slowly to Ryan's truck. A younger man moved his fists, as if to mime boxing someone, and was shushed by an older man near him. This was no time for tomfoolery.

The tense scene was at odds with the beautiful morning, with long rays reflecting from the placid seas into the undersides of clouds, painting them pink. Ryan looked over at the solemn men and realized he saw none of the Highliners. The back of his brain tingled with the sense of impending danger. *Why was that?* he asked himself. *Where were they?*

Ryan drove slowly, carefully. He knew he was arresting one of the best men on the island—hardworking, honest, scrupulous, always willing to lend a hand. If Liberty Island were an independent state, Caleb might well be its governor.

As Ryan's truck proceeded northward across the island, he saw some people standing in their driveways, their arms crossed, their countenances disturbed, some angry. An air of edginess hovered over the island. Word already had passed, Ryan realized. Caleb stared straight ahead and didn't say anything, but he could have listed the relationships as Ryan's truck went by: Aunt. Cousin. Cousin. Basketball teammate. Ex-sister-in-law. First girlfriend. High school math teacher. And so on. Of course, people had seen the FBI man's truck on the commercial wharf, parked there for well over two hours. Two or three trucks were moving along behind him, but that was normal—there was only one road off the island.

And then suddenly things were not normal. When he passed the flashing COFFEE/BEER neon of the Downeast Depot sign at the island's main intersection and began to roll down the hill to the causeway that led to the bridge to the mainland, a big red four-door Dodge Ram 1500 pickup truck pulled out in front of him and came to a stop, crosswise across both lanes of the blacktop. Its blinkers were flashing. Ryan braked. He looked into his rearview mirror and saw the second of the two trucks behind him swing into the left lane and stop.

He pulled his Glock from his ankle holster and stepped out of his truck, only to find the two side-by-side barrels of a shotgun staring at him from inches away. They looked huge.

"You put that down on the ground," a voice said from behind the weapon. Ryan recognized the voice from the café. He had heard it ordering the Hungry Man's Special—three eggs, three strips of bacon, three sausage patties, three pancakes, syrup, and hash browns. It was Guppy, one of the Highliners. Ryan did as ordered. "Now put your hands up." He did. Someone behind him slipped a hand into his pocket and withdrew the keys to his truck.

Herc stepped up. His next demand surprised Ryan. He yelled across the truck, "Caleb, now you get out."

Caleb declined. "No, I don't think so, Herc."

Herc insisted. "Caleb, I will shoot you if I have to. But you are not leaving this island in this man's truck."

Caleb's voice turned sharp. "Goddamn it, Herc, get over here," he commanded. His face showed anger and frustration.

Herc and Guppy walked around to the truck's passenger side. "I got a plan, Caleb," Herc said, an edge of pleading in his voice. Then, his voice dropping, he explained: "I take you to the *Sea Angel*. We drop this FBI man unharmed on an outer island with food and water for three days. We do an overnight run due east to Nova Scotia, the way our granddads did."

Caleb looked into Herc's excited eyes. "Look, I hear you, brother," Caleb said, almost consoling his friend. "And I appreciate what you are trying to do for me.

"But," he continued, "this is not the way to go. Obstructing justice, kidnapping a federal agent? That's gonna bring a world of shit down on the island, Herc."

Caleb explained, "You embarrass the federal government, they're gonna have to show us who's boss. Place would be crawling with feds. There would be no end of trouble. Fishermen only a step outside the law, maybe behind a couple years on their federal income taxes, would get knocks on the door in the middle of the night, told they play ball or lose their boats.

"The feds would wreck this place, Herc," Caleb said. The thought pained him, and that was clear from his face. "That's not what I want. So I need you and the boys to back off." Herc's broad, plain face considered the request. Guppy watched them both, waiting, mouth open, not knowing what to do next. In a sharper tone, Caleb added, "I mean now, right now, before things go way wrong. Herc, I've told him everything. He knows what happened. And this way, there are no warrants, no people getting unnecessarily frightened."

Herc stared at him, then nodded. "All right," he conceded. His shoulders sagged. He was crying a little from tension and grief. He reached into the cab and shook Caleb's hand. Then he walked back around the truck. "Give the man his keys," he ordered as he wiped at his eyes with a shirtsleeve. Guppy handed them to Ryan, along with his Glock. Someone else waved his arms outward at the big truck down the hill to signal it to clear the way. Ryan looked at Herc, Guppy, and the others. Their faces had crumpled from bold and defiant to befuddled and worried. Caleb's rebuke had planted new concerns: *What had they been thinking? And how would they get by without him?* More specifically: *Herc is a fine fellow, but was he the right fit to lead the Highliners, even temporarily, while Caleb was away?* Their world was wobbling on its axis.

Ryan stepped up into the driver's seat, then drove the truck down the hill toward the causeway. He remained silent for a bit, and finally said, "Thanks."

"No problem," Caleb said.

"Is there going to be any more trouble?" Ryan asked.

"Like from Herc and the boys?" Caleb asked. He shook his head slowly. "No. I don't hardly know anyone off island." Ryan thought he detected a bit of pride in that statement, like the fewer off-islanders someone knew, the better. He let it pass, satisfied just to know that there would be no more shenanigans.

Caleb looked over at Ryan. "You may laugh, but when I was a boy, I knew two old women who had never been off island. Not in their whole lives. One day I asked one of them how come, and she said, 'Everyone I know is here.'"

They crossed the causeway and then went up and over the tall suspension bridge, half a mile long. Life looked different from that mainland. The whole affair involving Ricky Cutts was about the island; it was always about the island and its ways. But the perspective shifted after they crossed the bridge. Ryan thought ahead: he would take Caleb to Bangor, have the marshals at the federal courthouse book him, order a takeout lunch for the two of them, and get a statement from him.

Booking someone on a federal charge is like checking someone into a hospital: it always takes far longer than anyone expects. In this case, it wound up taking most of the day and a bit of the evening. Time is the payment that bureaucracy demands as tribute.

First, Ryan gave Caleb his proper Miranda warning. Then he took a statement from Caleb, with a marshal as a witness. Ryan typed it up and gave Caleb a printout. "Make any fixes you like," he said, handing him a pen. Caleb made some small changes, and Ryan entered them. Then Caleb read it over again and signed it. Ryan had him read it aloud in front of a video camera. Finally, Ryan went down to his desk and called Harriet to say he had made an arrest and would follow up soon with a case report. "See, I'm not a basket case," he said, realizing as he said it that he sounded defensive. He still felt the sting of her comments about her lacking full confidence in him.

"Didn't say you were," she said dryly.

"But you worried about it," he said.

"You bet. Doing my job," she said. "Look, Ryan: What would you do if you found a troubled subordinate lying flat out on his back porch, comatose and incommunicado for well over a day?"

He considered that riposte. "I see your point," he said.

"Yeah," she said. "Good." They understood each other.

He went down to the basement to say goodbye to Caleb in his cell. He told him to get a good lawyer, "even if you think you don't need one."

Caleb said, "Do you understand now why I couldn't go to Ricky's wake?"

Ryan scratched an ear. "I'm thinking it's because it's bad luck to go to the wake of someone you've killed?"

"Yep," Caleb said, grinning. "Now you're thinking like a Maine fisherman."

On the way home under the stars and a sliver of a moon, Ryan turned on Hank Williams. The songs went by without him noticing much, until he found himself singing softly along: "I saw the light, I saw the light. . . . Praise the Lord, I saw the light." He had never before sung along with Hank.

He slept solidly and was up at first light. He opened his laptop and wrote his preliminary report on the case in three hours. At 8:58 A.M., he emailed it to Harriet. Two minutes later he called her. "I'm beginning to like Maine," he said.

She didn't say anything for a long moment. Then she counseled, "Ryan, you may want to experience a winter up there before you make any big decisions about staying. It can be a cold, dark world, just black and gray. Roads glazed with ice, the sun setting at three thirty on December afternoons. Then, in early February, you get wind chill numbers that almost make no sense. You look at it and think, 'Minus twenty-two, that must be wrong.' But it isn't. You eat, work, and sleep. That's it. It can feel like elemental survival."

Tell me about it, Ryan thought sarcastically. *That's a pretty good description of the world I've lived in for the last five months.* But all he said was, "Thanks, Harriet."

With a chiming ping, an email arrived from D'Agostino at the State Police. "Pretty good for a newcomer to the state—case closed in two weeks, start to finish, with a full confession."

Ryan felt better than he had in months. He called the grief counselor down in Hallowell the doctor had recommended and made an appointment. Then he went out onto the back porch with his second coffee. While he sipped it, he contemplated the motionless surface of the pond and the pines topping the low ridge on the far shore. Then he brought his eye back to the tiny ripples made by a turtle swimming just under the surface of the black, tannin-stained water. A chickadee on a branch next to the porch nodded and sent a friendly jabber his way. He took a deep breath of the piney air. It felt good.

Abby Buck's grim epitaph for Ricky Cutts came to his mind: *The world was now a better place.* Ryan wondered if the same could be said for Caleb Goodwin being behind bars. He honestly didn't know. But he had carried out his assigned mission and he had followed the law, and that was a start. Like Caleb, he had done his duty as he saw it. But he was beginning to think that sometimes our virtues can be as troublesome as our vices. And that some angels carry messages of death.

EPILOGUE

A SUMMER EVENING ON LOST POND

L ate one Saturday afternoon in mid-August, two months after
the Cutts case was closed, Ryan was sitting on his back porch,
reading a history of post-Revolutionary Maine, *Liberty Men and
Great Proprietors*. The title had caught his eye in a Brunswick bookstore. The contents went a long way toward explaining to Ryan why
the people who settled Maine harbored bitter feelings toward the
people of Boston. His mind drifted to Liberty Island. He wondered
who would fill Caleb's shoes in the Highliners, even just for the few
years the jury had given Caleb. Would the replacement be able to
keep Abby Buck in line? He'd heard that Caleb was running for
the island's school board from his jail cell. The warden had agreed
that, if elected, Caleb could attend meetings by Zoom. He made
a mental note that the next time he was in Thomaston, he should
visit Caleb in the state prison.

He heard the driveway gravel crunch and walked through
the cottage to see who was coming. Probably the UPS man,
he expected, who once again would make cranky jokes about

delivering to people living in the woods. "There oughta be an extra charge for you hermits," he once had grumbled to Ryan.

But when he opened his front door, he saw Solid Harrison, the high-end fish marketer from Rockfish, emerging from her blue Prius. She was carrying a grocery bag. And she was as alluring as ever, now dressed in tight jeans, ankle-high black boots, and a close-fitting suede jacket over a purple silk blouse. Her long brown hair tumbled down her back.

She walked to his door and smiled. "I brought you something," she said, leaning forward slightly so he could see into the bag she carried. He looked down and saw a bottle of white wine, water crackers, and a food container. "And," she said, "my homemade lobster salad."

"This is unexpected," he smiled. "I mean," he was quick to add, "an unexpected pleasure."

They stood and talked for a while, about this and that, just reacquainting. She was wearing perfume, which he loved on a woman. "I've been thinking of you ever since I ran into you at that bookstore," he said.

"Me too," she said. She could sense that he was about to offer her a drink—coffee or beer or wine, he would say. A look of impatience crossed her face. She put down the bag and took a step closer to him. "Put your arms around me," she said.

Hmm. *Okay*, he thought, and he did.

"Do you like that?" she asked, looking into his eyes.

"Yes," he said, "I do." It had been a long time. He always had liked the feel of a woman's body, how you instantly could tell it was different. He pulled her in close and enjoyed her warmth and fragrance. His fingertips felt her spinal ridge.

Her green eyes held his steadily. "Now, would you like to kiss me?" she asked.

Yes, he would. It was long and languorous. He stepped back, but kept his arms around her. "What about your partner?" he asked.

"My ex-partner," she corrected. She explained that Dorothy had told her she wanted to put their relationship on hiatus. "That was the word she used, 'hiatus.' I told her I am not a TV show. And I moved out." That was all a couple of weeks ago, she said. "This afternoon I was thinking about you, about how I found you attractive both times we met."

"And?"

"And I decided to act on it."

"I'm glad you did," he said, grinning. "Do you want to go on a date?"

Solid had decided she was too mature to beat around the bush. "Well, if you want to," she said, "but what I really want is for you to take me to bed."

He was momentarily taken aback. She smiled at the look on his face, then said, "The older I get, the blunter I become. Life is too short. I liked you when I met you, and I thought back then that if I were single, I'd make a play. And now I am."

And so he did.

He had never slept with a woman fifteen years older than himself. She was both lively and languid. She knew what she wanted and told him. Their lovemaking was unhurried and delightful. She had a long, shuddering orgasm that culminated with a yowl so loud it made him glad they were out in the country. When he began thrusting into her, she stuck her tongue in his right ear and said, "Slower, slowly, slow. Let my tongue be your controller. When I stick my tongue in, slowly, you follow that way, push in, slowly." He moved as gradually as he could, barely shifting his hips at times, while she whispered warmly into his ear between tongue flicks. Finally, after what felt to Ryan like an eternity but was really only about seven minutes, she said, "Now. Hard. Fast. Fill me up." Her tongue shot in and out of his ear, and then she bit his earlobe. He had an orgasm like hers, then buried his head in her shoulder.

"I never knew Maine could be so sexy," he finally said.

"Well, we have long winters," she said, a bit elliptically. "You got to get through them somehow."

The days that would bring blizzards were still far away, but the afternoon was cooling as the sun settled into the treetops, so when they went out on the back deck, he wore a sweatshirt and jeans while she wrapped herself in the unzipped sleeping bag he used as a bedcover. They talked, sitting shoulder to shoulder on a big wicker chair, looking not at each other but out over the lowering gleam of sunlight on the surface of the pond.

Their conversation felt as clear and open as the brilliant deep blue sky. "I, uh, thought you were a lesbian," he said. "Boy, was I wrong."

She chuckled. "That's a label," she said. "If you need one, I guess it would be 'bi.' I just know I am attracted to certain people, some female, some male." A loon's cry fluttered across the pond.

She opened the bottle of Sancerre while he laid out the lobster salad and crackers. She had roasted the lobsters on a grill and then mixed their meat with aioli, chopped bacon, and arugula. "This is wonderful," he said after a first bite and a sip of the crispy wine.

"Thanks," she said. "I only make it for special people."

"I meant I liked the salad, but I also meant having you here, and making love with you, and sitting out here taking in the sunset. It is all quite wonderful. I feel grateful and alive. I haven't felt that way in a long time."

"It's a good way to have a date, no? Have the sex first, then afterward there's less tension, less worry, and you can just relax and enjoy the moment with the other person." She looked again at him. "But why haven't you been grateful?"

"You need to know something about my life." He told her about his family, how he thought about Marta, Pablo, and Stefanie every day. Now he felt they were no longer hidden from him under white sheets.

She teared up as she listened and reached out to hold his hand. "I knew there was something. You had an uncertainty or sadness in your eyes, I couldn't tell which."

Later they talked about the difference in ages and what it might portend. "Right now, I feel like it is to our mutual advantage," she offered. "I'm attracted to your energy, and you seem to like my wisdom."

He said he liked her willingness to use that last word, to claim it as her own. "You seemed to sense," he said, "that I hadn't been with anyone since before my family's accident, and you led me through it, in a gentle and friendly way."

She chuckled and said she liked his choice of word, "friendly." "I think that's what we may have here, a sexual friendship. I've never liked that 'friends with benefits' line. It underestimates the power of the relationship. A sexual friendship is different from other friendships. More intense, more vulnerable. It's not just 'benefits,' it's a primal connection."

He asked her where he thought this new relationship would lead. "Let it grow, don't put too much weight on it," she finally said. "We are two people who have found each other at the right moments in our two lives. How long will it last, and where will it go? Who knows? That's the fun part, but also the scary part. The Greeks said we walk backward into the future. I think that's certainly true of relationships."

A bright white half-moon began to move over the spruce and fir trees on the eastern side of the pond. He thought of it rising also over Liberty Island, nearly fourscore miles to the south. May its soft light bless that strange and lovely island, he thought.

ACKNOWLEDGMENTS

I am grateful to Cullen Murphy and George Gibson, two fine editors who helped this book come to life. My island author friends Kathryn Lasky and Katherine Hall Page also provided helpful thoughts and encouragement, as did my wife, Mary Kay Ricks, and my children, Chris and Molly. Another terrific novelist from a larger island, Adrian McKinty, also generously provided a helping hand.

In addition, I was inspired by the work of several Maine authors, most notably by Elizabeth Strout, Richard Russo, and Timothy Cotton. I also learned a lot from James Acheson's thoughtful and closely observed *The Lobster Gangs of Maine*, which I first read fifteen years ago, before I ever hauled a lobster trap, and then a second time while I was writing this book. Also, after writing this book I reread the wonderful book *The Lobster Coast* by Colin Woodward and realized how much I had absorbed from it.

Also during the time when I was writing this, I was encouraged daily by lovely photographs posted on Facebook by several photographers specializing in scenes of Maine landscapes and wildlife, among them Laura Zamfirescu, Laura Casey, Cassie Larcombe, Gary Vanidestine, Anastasia Webb, Donna

Hutchins, Jean Dube, Carl Duney, Jan Arabas, Brenda Ketch, Lance Macmaster, Rick Harder, Susannah Warner, Bob Warner, Bill Thomson, Lisa James, Sheila Wakefield, Myrna Clifford, Alex Pietro, Steve Yenco, Tony Palumbo, Tammy Black, Lori Denise, Kerry Nelson, Michael Facik, Carl Walsh, Sarah Lathrop, Mike Scott, Justin Venneman, David Luther, Teri Hardy, Stacey Feldmus, Paula Dysart Joy, Jeanne Skuse Peshin, Marcy Pluznick-Marrin, Kathleen Bowers-Pinette, Barbara Jackson-Garbarino (queen of loon portraiture), Helen Webster Drake, Donna Dodge Baker, Sue Ann Lane, Sarah Hope Hampton, Lisa Jordan James, Jill Turner Odice, Lee Ann Henry, Jessica Williamson Smith, Melanie Knaut-Stanley, Malcolm Ritter, Robert Smith, Wayne Smith, Clark Smith, Victoria Smith, A. G. Evans, Carl Walsh, Jack Zievis, Cindy Willigar, Bumpa Hennigar (what a great name), Dave Cleaveland, Mark Rowe, Keith Googines, Mark Rowe, Guy DeWitte, Louise Natale, Gudrun Heald, Courtney Laws, Albert Shepherd, William Pead, Angela Archer, Dick Marston, Bayleigh Jade, and C. F. Daniels. Dozens of times I thought to myself, "That image would look wonderful on the front of this book." Unfortunately, books usually only have one cover. In my ideal world, we'd do different covers of this book featuring the works of all these photographers.

Thanks also to Jessica Case at Pegasus Books for her deft editing of the manuscript. I am also grateful to Claiborne Hancock and Meghan Jusczak at Pegasus.

The mistakes, as always, are my own.